UNCHAINED VENGEANCE

ALSO BY MARK ALLEN

UNCHAINED VENGEANCE

LUCAS STONE
BOOK 4

MARK ALLEN

WOLFPACK
PUBLISHING
— EST 2013 —

Unchained Vengeance
Paperback Edition
Copyright © 2024 Mark Allen

Wolfpack Publishing
1707 E. Diana Street
Tampa, FL 33610

wolfpackpublishing.com

Paperback ISBN 978-1-63977-524-8
eBook ISBN 978-1-63977-523-1
LCCN 2024937437

"Fear him who can destroy both soul and body in hell."

MATTHEW 10:28

"But I say to you that everyone who is angry with his brother will be liable to judgment, and whoever says, 'You fool!' will be liable to the hell of fire."

MATTHEW 5:22

"And if your hand causes you to sin, cut it off. It is better for you to enter life crippled than with two hands to go to hell, to the unquenchable fire."

MARK 9:43

UNCHAINED VENGEANCE

PROLOGUE

WITH THE WEEKEND coming to an end, the prisoner returned to the top tier of his cell block at the United States Penitentiary in Lompoc, California, and thought about what somebody might look like with a knife sticking out of their eye.

He had just finished his mandatory work assignment—slave labor, when you boiled it down to the bare truth, and how it was still legal in America was beyond his comprehension—in the prison library. His job there was to pass out dogeared books, mop the floor with a bucket of dirty water, or scrub the graffiti-etched toilet, depending on what mood the on-duty Education Specialist was in. Some of them were all right, but the middle-aged whore who had recently been dumped by her boyfriend was in the habit of taking out her anger on the inmate workers under her supervision.

He had fantasized about killing her more than

once. Just shove her head in the toilet bowl, cut her throat open, and watch the water turn red. Leave her bled-out body for one of the COs—correctional officers —to stumble over during their rounds.

But of course, this was prison, where fantasy rarely evolved into reality.

Tonight, instead of joining the other inmates for evening recreation, he loitered behind in his cell. The correctional officer babysitting the block didn't pay him no mind, he skipped recreation more often than not, preferring the quiet solitude of a half-empty cell block to the chattering noise and never-ending posturing of the rec yard.

Even inside the cell block, he avoided the card games, domino tables, or the groups clustered around the TVs in their flimsy plastic chairs watching the raciest movie they could find on basic cable, half of them with their hands deep in their pockets and not even trying to be subtle as they played with themselves. You would think most of the morons in here were still in junior high the way they whooped and hollered about tits and ass on the television.

If the Federal Bureau of Prisons ever really wanted to control the inmate population, they should just give them free porn and stand back while the convicts jacked themselves into post-orgasmic comas six times a day.

His cellmate was currently doing sixty days in *the hole*—the slang term for the Special Housing Unit—for getting into a bare-fisted brawl with some Aryan Brotherhood bastards, so he had the cell all to himself.

Usually he just sprawled out on his bunk, cursed the paper-thin mattress that he still wasn't used to even after all these years on the inside, and enjoyed the isolation. If he was really bored, he cracked open a paperback and tried to lose himself in a fictional world.

But not tonight.

Tonight was different.

Tonight, it was time to kick the long-gestating plan into violent motion.

Eight months of meticulous planning, of hashing out every little detail, were about to pay off. His patience would be rewarded, the fires of bitterness he had stoked for all these years finally allowed to erupt into an inferno of retribution. He would taste freedom again, hunt down the traitorous bitch who had put him behind bars, and make her pay dearly for what she had done.

She might have forgotten him, but he had not forgotten her. After being caged up in this hellhole for so long, freedom would taste oh so sweet, but not as sweet as getting his hands on his ex-wife and exacting his revenge. He wasn't even sure what he was going to do to her yet, only that it would be as painful as possible.

He had made the phone call this afternoon, right after the mid-morning count and before the inmates lined up to shuffle down to the dining hall. All he had said to the person on the other end was, "Get ready, it happens tonight. You know where to be and you know what to do. Don't fuck it up."

"My middle name ain't *fuckup*," the person had said and promptly hung up the phone.

Alone in his cell, Jack *Lucky Draw* Dawson stared at his reflection—still handsome as hell, if he was being egotistically honest—in the warped, rippled polycarbonate prison mirror and reflected on his past, the checkered road of wealth and power that had eventually brought him here. He'd been a Las Vegas mob boss, living like a cutthroat king in Sin City, running a flourishing criminal empire of gambling, drugs, prostitution, and the occasional—but only when absolutely necessary—murder. He had no regrets, save one.

Marrying that worthless, backstabbing whore.

That's what I get for trying to do the honorable thing, he thought. *What kind of stupid slut gets pregnant from a one-night stand anyway? I should have put a bullet in her head and dumped her body in the desert instead of marrying her. Coyotes and vultures would have made her disappear in no time.*

He had no doubt that his ex-wife was in the Witness Security Program—WITSEC—after testifying against him and putting him away for the past decade. But that wouldn't stop him from hunting her down, killing her as slowly as possible, and then taking his daughter and hightailing it to some non-extradition country. No doubt his daughter hated him by now, but she would learn to love him, in all the right ways. Or rather, all the *wrong* ones. And if she fought him, if she didn't get with the program...well, then she could meet the same fate as her worthless mother.

Yeah, tonight's the night. Fuck this place and everyone in it. Time to get the hell out of here.

He reached for the small red-and-white bottle of Tylenol on the stainless-steel shelf screwed to the wall below the mirror. He had purchased the bottle from the commissary last week and used it to hide the painkillers he'd bribed from the prison pharmacy technician down in health services. She was an annoying midget of a woman—seriously, didn't the Bureau of Prisons have a height requirement to get a job?—and about as round as two elephants standing side by side, but it was well known among the inmate population that she would sell you just about any medication for the right price.

He popped the painkillers, washing them down with a shot of prison hooch he'd bought from the guys in the cell next door. There was no way he could go through with what had to be done without something to take the edge off the coming pain. The pills and the booze would help, but he still cringed at the thought of what was coming. But a little pain—okay, a *lot* of pain—was a price worth paying to regain his freedom and sanity and the chance at revenge.

On the shelf next to the bottle of Tylenol was a plastic toothbrush, its end sharpened to a point, thin and tapered without turning into a needle. More like a stiletto. In the state joints, the makeshift knife was referred to as a shiv, but inside the federal prison system, they called it a shank. He had no idea why, nor did he care.

Time unspooled in such a way that every second felt like a minute. The clock moved slower than a turtle trying to crawl uphill through molasses. Dawson paced the cell, prowling his concrete cage like a restless lion. He told himself to relax, even tried some deep breathing exercises, but it was a waste of time. He just wanted to get this whole thing over with.

At 2045 hours, just fifteen minutes before the prison locked everyone in their cells for the official headcount, inmates started drifting back from recreation and the noise level in the housing unit got jacked through the roof, easily quadrupling in volume. Dawson definitely wasn't going to miss this nightly cacophony of noise. He heard the correctional officer—Marvin Lindsey, was his name—shouting for them to shut up but nobody listened. What's the worst he could do, write them an incident report? The lieutenant on duty didn't want to deal with that crap and would just expunge it anyway.

At 2105 hours, Dawson started to steel himself for what needed to be done, the sacrifice he had to make. It was almost time to do the hard thing and kick the plan in motion. He knew Lindsey was a real stickler for the rules, the kind of guard who didn't let anything slide and would do his job by the book. Some correctional officers succumbed to laziness or complacency and just pretended to count, but Lindsey would shine a flashlight into each cell and force each inmate to show himself—*"Gotta see living, breathing flesh,"* he would say if you complained—instead of just taking it for granted that there was an inmate under the blankets on the bunk.

He also wouldn't summon health services unless it was a serious situation. Tell him you had an upset stomach or a pulled muscle or something menial like that and he would just tell you to suck it up and make Sick Call in the morning. Dawson knew he needed to make sure Lindsey had no choice in the matter. When Dawson was done, the CO Lindsey would be calling for the on-duty nurse as fast as his fucking fingers could hit the transmit button on his radio. Failure to do so would be a serious dereliction of duty that would cost him his job, regardless of how good his union rep was.

The count was nearly finished. Lindsey had already completed his rounds on the other three tiers. Dawson heard the metallic jangle of the keys on Lindsey's duty belt rattling together as the CO approached the cell, calling out, "It's count time, boys! Show me some skin and let me know you're breathing."

You can do this, Dawson pep talked himself, looking at his reflection in the mirror again. The reflection stared back, letting him see the beads of cold, anxious sweat popping out on his forehead. *You have to do this. You don't have a choice. Not if you want out of here. There's no other way and just remember, on the other side of the pain is sweet, sweet freedom.*

He flashed a crooked smile at his reflection, then picked up the shank and, without hesitation, stabbed it into his left eye.

The point popped the vitreous orb in a gushing burst of milky fluid. Dawson screamed and dropped to the floor, his knees hitting the tile hard enough to leave bruises. He toppled onto his side and curled up in the fetal position, nausea gnawing at his guts. He heard Lindsey's footsteps pounding on the concrete outside as the correctional office rushed up to the window in the door. The guy had been around the block enough to know that a screaming inmate was not something to be ignored. The powerful flashlight beam filled the cell with harsh, white illumination, and Lindsey cursed as he saw Dawson writhing on the floor like a salted slug, bloody gore streaming from his punctured eye socket.

"Goddamn it, Dawson! You stupid son of a bitch!"

Dawson struggled to remain conscious through the white-hot pain, which was even worse than he had imagined. It felt like the painkillers hadn't actually killed a damn thing. He heard the guard utter another curse and key up his radio.

"Lindsey to Control, I've got a medical emergency up here. Repeat, a medical emergency. Inmate down and bleeding with what appears to be eye trauma. Need assistance ASAP."

Emergency tones went off like a banshee wail as whoever was manning the prison control center punched some alarm button to summon assistance to the cell block. Even through the intense pain, Dawson could hear the loud *Bee-beep! Bee-beep! Bee-beep!* of the alarm signal being transmitted to all radios in the prison.

He felt the blackness rushing up to claim him like some primordial beast surging from the abyss. The shadows circled at the edge of his vision, the light dimming, the darkness coming to carry him away. The excruciating agony made it impossible to smile, as much as he wanted to.

Ready or not, here I come, motherfuckers.

It was all going exactly as he had planned.

———

THIRTY-NINE MINUTES LATER...

"I hear they call you Lucky," the EMT said. "I can see why. If that shank had gone in just a little bit further, you'd probably be talking to the angels right about now."

Or the devil, Dawson thought, opening his right eye —the only one he had left—as he emerged from unconsciousness. Light stabbed down at him, sharp and piercing, blurring his vision. *Oh, man, that hurts.* The painkillers he'd swallowed an hour ago didn't seem to be doing much to dull the pain. Maybe he should ask for some morphine. The light seemed to lance right through his skull like a laser drill. In fact, a drill through the brain might be preferable right now, at least then he would be out of his misery.

He was face up on a gurney in the back of an ambulance, as far as he could tell, ankles shackled by leg irons and his wrists restrained by handcuffs. The EMT loomed over him, a pretty young brunette that reminded him of his ex-wife but without all the traitorous baggage.

The guard, Lindsey, rode beside him, now strapped with a Smith & Wesson 9mm pistol and three spare magazines bristling on his belt. He wore a black Kevlar vest and a Federal Bureau of Prisons badge dangled from a chain around his neck, making him look very official.

Dawson knew there would also be a chase vehicle following the ambulance, with at least one more guard armed with not only a pistol but an M-16 carbine and Remington twelve-gauge pump-action as well. The carbine would be loaded with 5.56mm rounds, and the shotgun would have a tube full of buckshot shells.

Trying to shake off the pain, Dawson realized his plan was still in motion.

So far, so good.

"What the hell happened, anyway?" the EMT asked him. She sounded both concerned and curious. Dawson wondered if this was her first prison run.

The pain was brutal. Dawson ignored her question and instead asked one of his own. "How bad is it?" The drugs slurred his speech a bit, but that was the least of his worries.

"You'll live," the pretty little EMT replied, "but that eye is a goner."

"He'll live?" Lindsey snorted with derision and disappointment. "That's too bad, because I was really hoping the bastard would die. You know what this son of a bitch tried to do to his daughter before his wife turned on him and sent him to prison? If he wasn't protected by the mob, the inmates would have shoved a broken broom handle up his ass every damn day and twice on Sundays."

"I don't want to know all the gory details of his life," the EMT said, preparing a syringe. "To me, he's just another patient." She looked down at Dawson, and once again, he thought of his wife. "This is going to knock you out, so just sit back and enjoy the oblivion."

I could say the same to you, Dawson thought. *Sorry, lady.*

Before the EMT could sink the needle into his flesh, an explosion rocked the night like hell's own thunder.

————

Nate Parker had been employed with the Federal Bureau of Prisons for just under eight years, coming in the door as an entry-level GL-5 correctional officer before rising to the rank of Senior Officer Specialist in near-record time due to his work ethic, intelligence, leadership abilities, and willingness to work any post. Not just the cushy, air-conditioned ones like Control Center or Perimeter Patrol, but the less-desirable posts like Suicide Watch or any of the other crappy details usually reserved for rookies. To Parker, an eight-hour shift was an eight-hour shift and he didn't much care where he worked it.

That being said, his favorite assignment was Medical Escort Officer, which let him get out of the prison to take inmates to the hospital when their injuries or illnesses were beyond the basic triage capabilities of health services. Grab a chase car, pistol, and shotgun, and get rolling down the road behind the ambulance.

Like right now.

I can't believe Jack "Lucky Draw" Dawson got stabbed in the fucking eye. Guess the poor bastard wasn't so lucky tonight.

Parker was neither an inmate-hater nor a hug-a-thug, remaining neutral in his dealings with the convicts in his charge. But even if Dawson deserved what he got, a shank in the eye had to suck, and Parker lowered his usual shield of indifference long enough to feel a pang of sympathy for the mobster.

The ambulance in front of him, framed in the headlights, veered onto a secondary road that would loop them around to the hospital while avoiding the main highways. Parker easily kept pace in the chase car, and even though it wasn't required, he flipped on the emergency lights. Red-blue pulses strobed the darkness and reflected off the back doors of the speeding ambulance.

He kept his hands on the wheel, his eyes on the road, and half his brain focused on the job at hand. But the other half was thinking about a different kind of job, one that started with the word *blow*. He was having a torrid affair with the Medical Records Technician down in health services, a short brunette with sultry eyes and a great ass that made up for her mosquito-bite breasts. It had been nearly two weeks since they had been together and Parker ached to do ungodly things to her body that were still illegal in seven states.

Her husband worked at the prison too, in the Correctional Systems department—and outranked Parker by two grade levels—so there would be hell to pay if they ever got caught. Her husband wasn't a physically intimidating man, more scholar than fighter, but he had enough clout to make their lives miserable. Thing was, they weren't being that discrete, and Parker mentally chastised himself for their continued stupidity. Sometimes they acted like they wanted to be caught.

Nothing good ever comes from thinking only with your dick. Gotta use your brain sometimes, too.

She had promised to leave her husband—everyone at the prison, including half the inmates, knew their marriage was a joke—but so far, she had not pulled the trigger. Watching her go home with him every day after work drove Parker a little nuts. He didn't know whether to push the issue or just enjoy the ride while it lasted.

The explosion drove all thoughts of the affair right out of his head.

He slammed the brakes and cranked the wheel to the left, sending the chase car into a rubber-screeching slide as the blast lifted the ambulance into the air and flipped it on its side. Sparks shot into the night from the metal grinding on asphalt as the vehicle skidded down the road. As the chase car shuddered to a stop, Parker's rattled brain didn't fully register what was happening.

Then the three masked men emerged from the drainage ditch on the side of the road with SCAR assault rifles in their hands.

Shit! It's an ambush!

Parker clawed for the pistol holstered at his side but it was trapped by the seat belt.

The gunmen opened fire. The muzzle flashes looked like demonic eyes winking in the night.

Parker died screaming.

The hailstorm of bullets blew apart the car's windows and shredded the bodywork. Broken glass and sizzling lead whipped through the air like a vortex of destruction.

High-velocity rounds ripped into Parker's chest but were stopped by his Kevlar vest. He thrashed under the hammering impacts until the auto-fire tracked upward, seeking softer targets. The hot slugs tore apart his neck, face, and head, killing him instantly.

————

Dawson felt the ambulance flip onto its side as if backhanded by the fist of God. He, Lindsey, and the EMT went flying as glass shattered, bouncing around like rag dolls. Noise, smoke, fire, and debris filled the vehicle as it skidded down the road with the deafening screech of tortured metal.

As it slid to a stop, Dawson heard the chugging of automatic gunfire outside. His men apparently had not felt the need to use sound-suppressors this far off the main drag. Dawson knew the night air outside would be a seething maelstrom of hot lead. The men had been told to take no chances and would be in overkill mode. Dawson smiled despite his considerable pain, lips peeling back from his teeth in a sharkish grin. Anyone who saw that look would know they were dealing with a heartless, ruthless man.

He couldn't see outside the crippled ambulance yet, but he envisioned his men—masked and heavily armed—hitting the prison chase car first, slaughtering the backup guard, whoever he was. That much firepower had probably turned the officer into a blood-bursting piñata in just a few seconds, riddling his body with dozens of bullets. He could collect his next paycheck in hell.

That just left Lindsey to deal with.

The correctional officer was trying to free himself from the debris, arms and legs kicking like a turned-over turtle. The EMT was unconscious and sprawled on top of him, pinning him down like a wrestler trying to win a match, their limbs all tangled up. "Wh-what's going on?" Blood streamed from a gash in his temple that would require stitches if he lived long enough.

Not that Dawson had any intention of letting that happen.

Another burst of auto-fire, this time from the front of the ambulance. The driver cried out a high-pitched, agonized scream as bullets ripped the life out of him.

Lindsey looked shocked, horrified, and enraged.

"I knew you were up to something, you bastard!" he snarled at Dawson, his face red with exertion as he struggled to shove the unconscious EMT off him. He managed to shift her enough that he was able to reach for his pistol, but his hand groped at nothing. The holster was empty. The gun had shaken loose when the ambulance flipped over and sent its occupants tumbling around.

The back door flew open as Lindsey scrambled to find his pistol, crawling toward the front of the ambulance. The three gunmen wasted no time in cutting him down, all of them firing short bursts into his back, just below the Kevlar vest. The bullets angled up through his torso and exploded from his chest in a grisly series of exit wounds. The brutal impacts hammered him facedown and flat.

"Find his cuff key and get these fucking chains off me," said Dawson. He could almost taste the freedom, it was so close at hand.

One of the gunners climbed into the ambulance, patted down Lindsey's corpse until he found the thin metal key clipped to the man's nylon duty belt, and quickly freed Dawson from the shackles. Once the restraints fell away, the mob boss picked up Lindsey's fallen pistol. It had been a long time since he had held a gun and it felt good. It looked like a Smith & Wesson but he couldn't be sure—his vision was all messed up. Stabbing yourself in the eye will do that to you. Not that the make and model of the gun really mattered, as long as it got the job done.

His finger slid through the trigger guard and took up the slack. He could feel the cold steel wanting to break, to snap back and send a bullet blasting from the barrel. After a decade of being told what to do in that shithole of a prison—where to stand, where to eat, where to sleep, hell, even where to take a crap—it felt damn fine to be in charge again. Despite the pain in his eye—or rather, the mangled remains of his eye—he felt good. Power and control were fantastic anesthetics.

He looked down at Lindsey. The correctional officer was sprawled on his stomach in a huge pool of blood, his lower back chewed into ragged meat by the bullets that had brought him down. Dead, no doubt about it. Nobody could soak up that much lead and live to tell the tale.

Still, Dawson wanted to be sure. Plus, his rage and pain needed an immediate outlet.

He stepped out onto the wreckage-strewn pavement and stretched for a second, rolling his shoulders, loosening up his muscles. Then he turned and shot Lindsey in the back of the head. The 9mm bullet blew off a chunk of skull and sent brain tissue splattering everywhere. The interior walls of the ambulance looked like they had been coated with bloody oatmeal.

"It's count time, Lindsey!" Dawson bellowed at the corpse. "In hell!" He shot the officer again, another bullet in the head for good measure, a gruesome coup de grâce. The by-the-book bastard might get buried with honors, but it for damn sure was going to be a closed-casket funeral. Nobody wanted to look at a hero with no face.

The EMT stirred, groaning her way back toward consciousness. She pushed her upper body off the floor, struggling to climb to her feet.

One of the gunmen jerked a chin in her direction. "What do you want to do with that pretty little thing?"

Dawson raised the pistol and shot her in the head too. "Bitch reminded me of my ex-wife. Good enough reason for her to die."

The four men retreated to a waiting transport, a black SUV. Moonlight shimmered on the waxed hood. They were long gone before any police or prison reinforcements arrived to clean up the mess.

Dawson smiled to himself. The plan had worked to perfection. The United States Marshal Service would launch a nationwide manhunt for him.

His smile withered as he thought of the person

who had betrayed him, the backstabbing bitch who had broken her vows and put him behind bars.

Yeah, let the marshals fumble along his trail, trying to catch up. He had some hunting of his own to do. Truth be told, he really didn't care all that much if he got caught as long as he got to see his ex-wife again first.

Because some debts need to be paid in person.

ONE

DEWEY YOUNG WAS DEAD, and Lucas Stone was not surprised. He *was* surprised Dewey had lasted this long, given his poor health and the hard, roughshod living he had indulged in most of his life. Giving your life over to God in your twilight years after a lifetime of recklessness wasn't a bad thing—if Stone believed in anything, he believed in redemption —but it wouldn't stop the heart attack coming with your name on it. Turning over a new leaf didn't shield you from the consequences of the old leaf.

The sins of Dewey's past could be found on his considerably long rap sheet. Most of the offenses were petty misdemeanors, but there was some serious, felonious stuff on there as well, ample proof that the man was no saint.

But Dewey's fingers could do more than commit crimes—his musical mastery of the organ, piano, and keyboard were nothing short of magical. Shortly after Dewey started attending Faith Bible Church, Stone had made him the organist. Dewey had quickly eschewed contemporary praise and worship tunes in favor of updated renditions of the classic melodies found in the hymnbook.

In Dewey's hands, "All Creatures of our God and King" became a panegyric. He blew the dust off "Crown Him With Many Crowns" and enlightened the metrical accents. His bluesy, honky-tonk version of "Amazing Grace" was a minor sensation that quickly went viral in the tri-lakes region via texts and social media shares. The local newspaper ran an article on him and the public radio station interviewed him live on the air. The size of the small congregation nearly tripled in just a few weeks as people came to see the reformed criminal turned organ magician.

Stone was more of a rock 'n' roll guy but he could listen to Dewey play for hours. The man simply knew how to summon magic from the keys, like he was some kind of organ whisperer. Stone knew the surge in congregational numbers was because of Dewey, not his preaching, but he didn't care. Whatever a person's reason for putting their butt in a pew, he was happy to have them. It was his job to preach the Word, not to question motives. In his opinion, *judge not* was one of the least obeyed commands in the Bible.

This was the first Sunday since the heart attack had knocked Dewey off the organ bench for good. They had buried him yesterday at the cemetery just up the road from the church, and somebody had even live-streamed the ceremony as if Dewey was some kind of celebrity. Stone didn't care about that kind of notoriety for the man, he just hoped

Dewey was in a better place after a lifetime of hellish living. Maybe up in heaven playing some ragtime on the piano while the angels boogied around him.

After the morning worship service, Rachel Gibson cornered him during the fellowship hour. He saw her coming as he drained the last of his coffee, which had gone cold because he spent more time talking than drinking. He tossed the Styrofoam cup into the nearby trash can before turning to greet her.

"Good to see you, Rachel," Stone said. She was a trustee on the Whisper Falls Town Board, elected to a four-year term shortly before Stone rode into town. He wasn't much for politics, but being the sheriff, he got to know people. Rachel could be snippy and pushy in equal measures but was generally harmless. "Hope you found the service to your satisfaction."

"My personal opinion, you're a better sheriff than preacher," Rachel replied, giving him a crooked grin that let him know she was only half serious. "But I was raised Episcopalian, so that may be coloring my judgment. Don't hold it against me."

"Father Andy over at St. Luke's in Saranac Lake does a damn fine job," Stone said, then followed up with a smirk. "For an Episcopalian, anyway."

"You're incorrigible. And you shouldn't swear in the Lord's house."

"It's just a building."

"Yes, well, it's a building that's missing Dewey Young's musical charms."

"I don't disagree with you," Stone replied. "But I can't bring him back from the dead and last time I checked, Jesus wasn't doing any more resurrection miracles. You got another solution?"

Rachel beamed. "I'm so glad you asked. We've had a real stroke of luck. Or a blessing, I guess you might call it. One of the music teachers over at the Lake Placid Center for the Arts has agreed to give us a discount on piano lessons for whoever we choose to send. You do know the LPCA would like to open an annex campus right here in Whisper Falls, don't you?"

Rachel was very big on boosting the local economy. It was one of her favorite platforms and she brought the subject up frequently, both in formal interviews and friendly conversation. Personally, Stone thought too much expansion would ruin the small-town flavor of Whisper Falls and rob it of its rural appeal. But he also recognized that stagnation could also kill off a small mountain town. It was a balancing act that he was happy he didn't have to figure out.

"Better a music school than a strip club like the one Bloomingdale is gonna get, I guess," Stone said. "I'm sure you heard."

Rachel looked like she had swallowed the world's sourest apple. "Don't even get me started on that travesty. I can't believe they're going to allow that kind of sleazy entertainment—if you can call it that—into our town."

"Not our town," Stone corrected. "Bloomingdale is five miles away."

"Close enough. *Too* close."

"Hell, it's not even our county."

Rachel shot him a sharp look. "I know you pride yourself on being some kind of worldly, unorthodox

headed into his office. He left the door open a crack but closed enough to give him some privacy. He wasn't really in the mood for company right now. All that thinking about the past on the drive over here had left him with a troubled mind and restless spirit. Or, hell, maybe he just needed another cup of coffee. Caffeine could cure a whole lot of ills.

Stone sat in his chair and reflected on all the wrong turns in his life, the dark chain of events that had led him to this town. The blood and bullets of his warrior days. The death of Jasmine. The divorce from Theresa. The decision to turn his back on black ops to become a preacher. The bleak realization that it wasn't so easy to leave the violence behind. The constant struggle to balance his desire to be a righteous man with his deep, burning need for primal justice when confronted with evil. Sometimes the guilt of his vigilante methods slammed into his gut like a punch from a professional boxer. He was supposed to save souls, right? Not gun them down for their sins.

Problem was, some people just deserved killing.

Stone pushed away the thoughts. They weren't doing him any good or offering any answers. For now, the warrior and the preacher personas lurking inside of him had managed to hash out an uneasy coexistence. The duality of his nature took its toll, but he was learning to live with it. He couldn't honestly say he was always at peace with his Jekyll and Hyde syndrome, but he made it work.

He muddled through the day with mundane office work that had been piling up, shuffling mostly unimportant papers that had been stacked so high that he never expected to see the bottom. By midafternoon, he'd had enough. Paperwork just wasn't his thing. His wrist ached so much from scribbling his name that it felt like he had been firing a .454 Casull revolver for eight hours straight. Since he'd come in early, he decided to leave early. Benefits of being the boss.

He told the day shift deputies to raise him by phone or radio if they needed him, then bailed from the office. Out in the Blazer, he called Holly and asked her to meet him for drinks and dinner at the Jack Lumber. Not a date—they didn't call it that, their relationship caught somewhere between platonic and romantic by mutual, unspoken consent—just a couple of good friends hanging out and helping each other through life. But Stone knew they couldn't keep doing the *maybe friends, maybe more* dance forever. Holly deserved a man who was all in, not one who kept her at arm's length…even if that's where she wanted to be right now.

Stone felt beaten down and drained but wasn't really sure why. He was generally even-keeled and not prone to depression, but today, he felt like there was some kind of darkness pressing down on him, like shadows on the horizon, brimming with danger and uncertainty. Spending some time with Holly would go a long way toward curing that, or at least taking the edge off. She knew many of his secrets and hadn't pulled away yet. Her smile could always brighten his mood, no matter how dark a day he was having.

Yeah, a damn good woman and I'm a fool for not making her mine.

The morning sun had been ambushed by thick,

swollen, angry clouds that had staked their claim on the heavens. As Stone started the truck, a few fat droplets splatted against his windshield like a warning volley, and then the skies opened up. The heavy thunderstorm began to drench the town as if trying to wash away all their sins.

———

NINETY MINUTES LATER...

Holly Bennett was late. Nothing unusual about that. She preferred to be early—she'd been raised on the "if you're not ten minutes early, you're late" mantra—but her preference and reality rarely synced up. And this damnable storm wasn't helping anything. It was a real doozy, the rain hammering down in sheets of liquid fury.

Drops of water struck her windshield like artillery shells, sounding hard as stones, as if they would break right through the glass and give the deluge access to flood the cab of her Jeep Gladiator. The wipers flicked back and forth at their maximum speed but just could not keep up. Saying it was coming down in buckets didn't do this rain justice. It had been a long time since she had seen a storm this bad, and she hoped it would be a long time before she saw it again.

Red taillights flickered ahead, vague smears of crimson. Cars inched down the soaked road at the speed of drying paint, fearful of hydroplaning. She couldn't blame them, but it still left her frustrated. *If you're too scared to drive, get off the road!* she wanted to yell, but of course, that wasn't fair. This storm had caught everyone off guard. Even the meteorologist on the news this morning had only predicted *"occasional spotty showers for the afternoon."*

She glanced at the dashboard clock and shook her head.

He'll just have to wait. I'll get there sooner or later.

A few minutes later, she turned the corner and saw the blue neon beer sign in the Jack Lumber's window blinking intermittently as if rattled by the storm. It was all blurry, like trying to read an eye chart at the bottom of a swimming pool after tossing back too many tequila shots.

The bar was situated on the town's main drag, wedged between a furniture store and liquor shop on each side. It was a nondescript establishment, a hangout for the locals rather than catering to the tourists. Holly drove past and pulled into the parking lot up the street, the rain pounding on the roof of her truck loud enough to make her deaf. She switched off the engine and pulled down the visor to check her face in the mirror.

Why? she asked herself. *It's not like it's a date or anything. Nothing is going to happen, and that's at least half your fault.*

Yeah, it was complicated.

Lightning flashed—a close one. It lit up the inside of Holly's Jeep and unleashed a crash of thunder that she felt deep down in her bones. A little smile creased her lips. How messed up would it be, after everything she had suffered and survived over the years, to get struck by a freak bolt of lightning? Stone claimed God had a sense of humor. Maybe it was a little more twisted than people gave Him credit for.

She reached into the back seat for her jacket and then muttered a curse when she realized it wasn't there. Lizzy must have borrowed it when she got dropped off at the school dance. The danger of being the same size as your teenage daughter was that she was always stealing your clothes. Holly shook her head in resignation, took a deep breath, and let it out, long and slow.

Looks like I'm about to get soaked.

She jumped out of the vehicle and dashed across the parking lot in the torrential downpour. The wind tried to pick her up and throw her across the border into Canada. She covered her head with her hands and just kept running, her boots splashing through deep puddles with every step, the rain slashing at her face like cold, liquid needles.

She reached the door to the Jack Lumber in less than twenty seconds, but that was all it took to drench her to the bone. She figured this was what it felt like when God flooded the world back in the day. Her wet blue jeans clung to her legs while the pink blouse she wore stuck to the upper half of her body.

When she went inside, the old black man with long scars on his face standing behind the bar let out a loud, appreciative whistle and called out, "Not saying I mind, but the wet T-shirt contest ain't 'til next weekend, sweetheart."

Holly smiled, shaking her head like a wet dog. "In your dreams, Griz, you dirty old man. A wet T-shirt contest would probably give you a heart attack."

"Yeah, maybe," the barkeeper conceded, teeth flashing white in a wide grin. "But what a way to go."

Holly made her way to the restroom to see if she could dry off, dripping a trail of water the entire way. When she looked in the mirror, her face flushed. Her soaked blouse was practically see-through, her bra blatantly visible beneath the sopping-wet fabric. No wonder she was getting looks from all the guys—and some girls—in the bar. Nothing like a free show! She wondered if Stone had seen her like this and immediately realized, of course he had. The bar wasn't that big, and Stone was not the kind of guy who missed much.

Next she wondered if he had liked what he saw.

Good lord, girl, get a hold of yourself and stop acting like some hot-to-trot hussy.

She grabbed a handful of paper towels that were about as soft as 40-grit sandpaper and almost as absorbent. Seriously, it felt like they were made out of plywood and they wouldn't work for crap. She switched to toilet paper, scrubbing frantically, but only succeeded in covering herself with shredded fragments of tissue that looked like large clumps of dandruff clinging to her wet clothes. Another glance in the mirror confirmed what she already suspected—that she still looked like a drowned rat.

Holly sighed in resignation and shook her head at her reflection. *Screw it. Nothing else you can do about it now. Can't let it ruin the evening.*

She brushed off as much of the toilet paper clumps as she could and headed out into the bar. She kept her head up and refused to feel embarrassed, vowing to look any leering drunk right in the eye and ask them what their problem was.

But as it turned out, the small crowd was no longer interested in her. She had spent enough time in the bathroom to become old news. They were now gathered around two men who were arguing loudly, their voices boisterous and angry. Looked like a fight was about to break out any moment, the intense violence of the storm outside giving birth to violence inside. She didn't worry about it too much, Grizzle had a shotgun loaded with rock salt beneath the bar that stopped most fights in their tracks and Stone was more than capable of breaking up a disturbance using his badge, his words, or his fists.

As she maneuvered through the crowd, she saw one of the men was Preston Daggett, the county historian, and the other was Steve Lepper, a local businessman who boasted a tattoo on his left wrist of a cigar-chomping leprechaun wielding dual Micro Uzis like Chuck Norris in *Invasion U.S.A.* Whenever someone asked Lepper about it, he claimed he was part Irish and the tattoo was his way of honoring his ancestors.

The two men were in a heated discussion about something, but Holly ignored them and made her way to where Stone sat in a booth in the back corner of the room, near the jukebox cranking out a Bon Jovi ballad about a bed of roses. She wondered if Stone had put it on, since he had a thing for classic rock, especially old-school hair metal. His playlists were loaded with bands like Cinderella, Def Leppard, and Poison.

He sat there with his rugged good looks, honey-colored eyes, and warm smile, and she found herself wondering—not for the first time—if it was time to lower the shields around her heart and take their friendship to the next level. Sure, they had settled into a comfortable familiarity with each other, but Holly knew better than most that comfort wasn't always enough.

She slid into the booth across from him, a little self-conscious about how she looked. "Sorry I'm late," she said.

He swirled his Jack and Coke. Most of the ice had melted. He gave her a little shrug. "No big deal."

Holly reached across the table and touched his hand. "No, really, I'm sorry. Lizzy had a dance tonight, and then the rain…"

He reached down and plucked a shred of toilet paper from her sleeve. "Must be true what they say—rain is just heaven flushing its toilet."

She smiled. "Not my best day, that's for sure."

"Looks like you could use a drink."

"I'm good for the moment." She gestured at the crowd gathered around Preston and Daggett. "What's all that ruckus about? Sounds like they're about to start swinging any second now."

"They're arguing about the strip club. Speaking of which…" Stone flashed her a grin. "…you look like you were getting ready to audition for the place."

"Very funny." Holly self-consciously folded her arms across her chest, doing her best to cover up the blouse that the rain had made see-through. "And seriously, a strip club? Maybe I'm wrong or just old-fashioned, but that seems like the last thing this place needs."

"Lepper wants to build one where the old Norman's Market is in Bloomingdale," Stone said. "That doesn't sit well with Daggett, who is hell-bent on keeping the old market untouched and designated as a historical site."

"Good for him. That's the right call. Norman's was there for over a hundred years."

"One hundred and ten, from what I hear."

"Plenty long enough to deserve better than getting turned into a strip club."

The two men opted at that moment to escalate from angry words to angry shoving, encouraged by the drunk—or at least drinking—people pressing around them. Some of the bystanders pushed the men into each other while others loudly urged them to fight. Cheers and insults filled the air in a volatile mix.

"You going to mosey over there and break that up?" Holly asked, thinking that maybe it was time for a drink after all.

"A shoving match?" Stone shook his head. "No, I'll let it ride for now."

"Aren't you the sheriff?"

"That's what the badge says."

"Not to mention a preacher," Holly added.

"You want me to slap cuffs on them or say a prayer?"

She glanced over her shoulder at all the pushing and jostling and swearing, then turned back to him. "The way things are going, you might have to do both."

"There's a time and place for everything," Stone said.

Grizzle came out from behind the bar and bulled his way through the crowd to confront the two men. He managed to look both stoic and pissed at the same time. "All right, you blithering idiots, that's about enough of this nonsense. This is a bar, not a boxing ring. You want to whip each other's asses, take the show outside. Otherwise, shut up, go back to your drinks, and mind your own damn business."

It was a good speech, but Daggett and Lepper ignored him. They both had their feathers way too ruffled to listen to a reasonable voice tell them to calm down.

"How can you disgrace Norman's like that?" Daggett demanded. "The place is a historical landmark in the tri-lakes area! It deserves better than to be turned into a sleazy strip joint so you can peddle tits and ass to lonely shmucks who can't get laid in real life."

"Who said it'll be sleazy?" Lepper retorted. "I plan on running a classy joint."

"You're calling it the Spicy Taco, for god's sake!"

"It's going to have a Mexican theme. All the girls will wear sombreros, and if you order six enchiladas, you get a free lap dance."

Daggett shook his head. "You're disgusting, man."

"And you're a prude," Lepper snapped. "Grow up, will ya?"

Just as Grizzle was about to lay hands on the two men and toss their butts out into the rain, Elissa Daggett slid effortlessly through the crowd and grabbed her husband's arm, pulling him away. She was a petite woman who was well into middle age, but she still had a tiny waist and curves in all the right places. She had been a stripper up in Canada during her younger days, dancing at a high roller gentlemen's club in Montreal, which was where she had first met Daggett. She was still a looker who could turn the head of just about any heterosexual male she walked by, but time was starting to catch up to her, as it did to everyone. The only way to escape old age was to die young.

"You two morons are supposed to be friends," she said. "Instead, you're acting like a couple of damn fools and making a scene. Stop the nonsense, settle down, forgive and forget, and all that crap, before Grizzle gives you both a lifetime ban from his bar."

The two men grumbled and grunted but begrudgingly backed down, much to the chagrin of the crowd that had been expecting a good old-fashioned brawl.

"Listen, Steve," Daggett said. "I'm heading out in the morning to the Widow Unser's farm to do some hunting. There's plenty of land there, so why don't you tag along, see if we can put some venison in the freezer?"

Lepper seemed to recognize the offer for the olive branch that it was. He straightened his shirt, accepted a bottle of beer that someone handed him, and looked at Daggett holding hands with Elissa. With a crooked grin and shake of his head, he said, "Sure, why not? A little hunting sounds good. This storm is going to turn the ground to mud deep enough to drown a pig, but what the hell. I'll see you out at the farm, crack of dawn, and if you're late, I'm taking your favorite stand."

Stone turned away from the drama and looked at Holly. "Guess I won't need those cuffs or prayers after all."

"Not so fast, cowboy. The night's young."

She left him on his own again to fetch herself a glass of wine from the bar. When she got back, the Daggetts and Lepper were leaving the bar together. All three were laughing and joking, as if the argument a few minutes ago had never happened. Looked like the two men were taking Elissa's advice to forgive and forget.

"So, what are your thoughts on having a strip club in this town?" Holly asked Stone as she slid back into the booth across from him.

"Not this town," Stone said. "Bloomingdale. Five miles away. Hell, that's not even Garrison County."

Holly sipped her wine and shrugged. "Close enough." She tilted her head to the side. "You saying you don't care?"

"I think it's up to the people of that town to decide. Not my town, not my county, so not really my business."

"Right, because nobody from Whisper Falls or Garrison County will ever go there."

"Sure they will. Still doesn't make it my business."

"A preacher staying neutral about a strip joint." Holly smirked. "Whatever is the world coming to?"

"If it makes you feel better, Deacon White is up in arms about it. Wrote a letter to the editor and everything."

"Well, at least somebody in that church is right with God." Her smirk turned into a full-fledged grin. "Lord knows with a drinking, killing, swearing preacher running the place, somebody has to pick up the slack."

The corner of Stone's lip tugged upward in a bemused smile. "Anybody ever tell you that you say hurtful things?"

"My daughter, my ex-husband, and Deacon White when I turn him down for dates."

"White still believes God told him you'll be his wife someday."

"Well, God forgot to pass that message along to me, so I've got four words for Deacon White: cold day in hell."

Still bemused, Stone replied, "Like I said—hurtful."

Holly rolled her eyes. "Yeah, whatever. I did read his letter to the editor, though. The guy may be a thorn in your side and a pain in my ass, but he can articulate, I'll give him that."

"From what I'm hearing, seems like half the people around here support the club, the other half are opposed to it."

"I'm betting the opposing half are all women." Holly smirked. "I can't imagine most guys are opposed to having a place to go stare at naked girls."

"I'm sure some men are opposed, too," Stone said.

"Only you religious types."

"I'm not religious." Stone grinned. "And who said I have a problem with naked women?"

"You're incorrigible."

Stone swirled the remnants of his watered-down Jack and Coke around in his half-empty glass and changed the subject. "How's Lizzy these days?"

"Typical teenage girl. Hates me one minute, loves me the next. Lots of smart-ass attitude."

Stone smiled. "She gets that from you."

"Don't I know it. Like mother, like daughter." Holly sighed. "But the thing is, something's off with her these days, and I can't figure out what it is."

"What do you mean?"

"It's hard to explain. She's just...not right. Not quite herself. Something's eating at her, and she's keeping it all bottled up inside."

"Have you tried talking to her?"

"No, Luke, that never crossed my mind." She gave him an exaggerated eye-roll and then smiled to show she was just giving him grief.

"I deserved that," Stone said. "Dumb question."

She reached across the table and patted his hand. "It's fine, Luke, really. I know you're just trying to help. But Lizzy won't talk to me about whatever's going on." She paused, unsure of how her next words would be received. "It's times like this that I wish she had a father in her life."

"I might not be her father," Stone replied, "but I care about her. About both of you."

"Sorry if that came out wrong," Holly said hurriedly. "I didn't mean to sound like I want you to be her father."

"I know what you meant," Stone said. "Don't worry about it. I'll try talking to her."

She left her hand on his. It felt warm, comforting,

like it belonged there. The fact that he didn't pull away meant something, right? *What the hell are we doing?* she wondered to herself.

Aloud, she said, "Thanks, that'd be great. Who knows, maybe she'll open up to you and spill her guts. Most of the time I'm pretty sure she likes you better than me, anyway."

Stone grinned, merriment in his honey-colored eyes. "Who doesn't?"

She smiled back. "Screw you, cowboy."

"Is that an offer?"

She batted her eyelashes at him. "You wish. This heart is closed for business these days."

Then again, she thought, *sometimes the heart has a mind of its own.*

THREE

ELIZA 'LIZZY' Bennett sat in the shadows of the storm's aftermath, curled up in a wicker chair on the three-season porch with a heavy wool blanket wrapped around her to ward off the chill of the rain-soaked night. Despite the blanket, a shiver shimmied down her spine due to the dampness, but she didn't want to go back in the house just yet.

The school dance had been fine in a boring, stilted kind of way, but she just wasn't much in the mood for socialization, so she had bummed a ride home, craving some alone time. Days like this, she was sure she could go to prison and happily live in solitary confinement for the rest of her life, tucked away in some forgotten corner of the world, safe from its troubles.

She reached up and brushed a strand of black hair out of her face, making a mental note to scrub off her makeup whenever she decided to go back inside. The purple streaks she liked to accent her hair with were starting to fade and she made another mental note to book an appointment at the salon to get that corrected soon. Maybe she would indulge in a manicure too, see if that made her feel any better.

She had lived in Whisper Falls for a few years now, but it still didn't feel like home. For that matter, she didn't even feel like she *had* a home. A lack of stability was the unfortunate price you paid for being in the Witness Protection Program—or Witness Security Program, as it was officially called. Your life could be uprooted at a moment's notice, without even time to pack or say goodbye to anyone, if the United States Marshals Service decided that was the best course of action to keep you protected. Quality of life was less important to them than simply making sure you were alive. Made it hard to feel like anyplace was actually *home*.

Still, out of all the places they had lived, she liked this house better than most, maybe even best of all. Maybe it didn't feel like *home*, exactly, but it felt *homey*. Rural, with no neighbors nearby, a decent little fenced-in yard with a yellow birch tree that she sometimes sat under and read a book during the warmer months. Of course, it was only warm up here in the Adirondacks, like, four months out of the year. This was snow country and it sucked.

No snow tonight, but the rain had been awful. Thank God she had borrowed her mom's jacket so she managed to stay mostly dry. Now she sat on the porch and fired up a cigarette, listening to the last rumbles of thunder as the storm moved off into the distance. The tip glowed cherry-orange in the darkness, like a demonic eye flaring open. She didn't smoke all the time, mostly just when she was stressed, and right now she was stressed to the fucking max. Maybe the Marlboro would help, maybe it wouldn't, but she had to try something.

She gazed out across the lawn, at the raindrops glistening like dew on the brown, wilting grass and sucked in a lungful of smoke. She immediately started coughing. It had been a while since she lit up a cancer stick. But she hacked her way through it until she was able to take another drag, this one much better, and enjoyed the nicotine rush.

For a few flickering moments, her thoughts drifted to the brief memories she had of her father. No, not memories. Not really, anyway. More like broken fragments, jagged pieces of a past life that she could never quite fit together to make a whole picture.

It was all so damn frustrating.

She had been so young when her mom snatched her up and fled into the night. She knew her father had tried to molest and abuse her, at least according to her mother, but she had no recollection of the event. No psychological trauma for a therapist to scrape away at while charging $125 an hour. She also knew that her mother had done what she needed to do in order to protect them both, but that didn't stop Lizzy from wishing she knew her father the way other girls got to know their dads. Sometimes—like right now, sitting on this porch in the cold dark—it felt like she had gotten a raw deal.

Yeah, life isn't always fair, and that's the truth. Thanks for hooking up with an asshole, mom. Of all the guys in Las Vegas, you had to sleep with an abusive mob boss?

She pushed away the thoughts and turned her attention to the leather-bound journal in her lap. It wasn't her imprisoned, absentee father who was causing her all the stress and giving her a reason to smoke, it was the two names written on the page open in front of her.

Nova Macero

Petra Macero

"White trash psycho sluts," Lizzy muttered.

Their names were neatly printed in all caps and underlined, the letters unable to capture the hate she felt for the so-called Macero twins. Next to their names, she had scribbled KILL THESE STUPID BITCHES! in a jagged, thorny script meant to convey death, rage, and danger. In the margins, she had drawn a crude skull and crossbones. Maybe not her proudest moment, but that was how she was feeling these days, and she had never been one to censor what she wrote down in her journal.

She flipped back through the pages, some of them splotchy with tear stains, and reread some of her recent entries. Just yesterday she had jotted down the lyrics from a Cannibal Corpse song.

> They deserve to die
> Plans have been completed and the time is
>   drawing near
> Punishment will be relentless
> They deserve to die

Not her usual musical taste, but the band managed

to tap into the violent anger she felt, so she rolled with it.

As if in counterpoint to the death metal lyrics, a few days earlier, she had copied a couple of lines from Emily Dickinson, her third favorite poet after Edgar Allen Poe and William Blake.

> *Because I could not stop for Death*
> *He kindly stopped for me*

Beneath the Dickinson poetry was an abbreviated quote from Leo Tolstoy. Because Lizzy was nothing if not well-read, with diverse musical and literary interests. In fact, she was pretty sure this nonconformity was the reason she was being targeted by the Macero sisters.

> *Today or tomorrow...death will come...nothing will remain but stench and worm.*

Elsewhere in the journal were just random entries with random words in random fonts, colors, sizes. Well, actually, the words weren't all that random. They mostly consisted of things like death, hate, and killing, as if penned by the lunatic mind of a madman. Even a complete stranger reading the journal would not have much trouble deciphering the theme. This was written rage, scribbled fury, emotional wounds manifested in black ink.

Tears filled Lizzy's eyes as she closed the journal hard enough that it sounded like a slap. She threw her head back, stared up at the porch roof, and screamed at the top of her lungs—a primal scream, raw and angry and void of all hope. With no one around to hear her, she screamed until she could scream no more, until her tortured throat felt like it might start bleeding if she even tried. The tears on her face matched the rain on the grass.

Finally, exhausted, she went inside the house and climbed the stairs to her room, the wool blanket trailing behind her like a makeshift funeral shroud. She didn't bother turning on any lights. She didn't need them, didn't want them.

Because right now, the darkness felt like the only friend she had.

FOUR

STONE WAS FORCED to cut his not-a-date with Holly short when he got a call about trouble brewing over at the Nailed Coffin, a dive bar at the other end of town. He arrived just as Deputy Sanchez pulled up in her cruiser. Good, the Latino spitfire could be his backup and he was glad to have her. She could out-brawl half the men he knew.

Inside, the place looked like any other unsavory hangout where cheap booze flowed in the front and drugs and illicit gambling went down in the back. The bar was to the right, a few rickety tables to the left, fly-spackled neon beer signs buzzing in the windows, and a small stage where a solo guitarist was currently cranking out a godawful rendition of an Aerosmith tune. The guitar was clearly out of tune and at least every third note the guy played was wrong. Stone had been called here several times before, but the stage—and the guitarist—were new additions. If it was an attempt to class up the joint, it was a failure.

The trouble came in the form of a tall, rawhide-and-bones man named Vance Macero, who was apparently a mean drunk who refused to leave when the bartender cut him off. Macero had a mop of greasy brown hair crowning his head, narrow eyes similar to Clint Eastwood's permanent squint, and crudely inked prison tattoos running down both arms. He looked to be in his late thirties, maybe early forties, and every one of those years had been hard.

"That hombre looks meaner than a pissed-off rattlesnake," Sanchez muttered.

"I've dealt with rattlesnakes before." Stone reached up and tapped the hatband on his Stetson before he stepped forward and said, "Closing time for you, Vance. Time to call it a night."

Macero had been leaning his elbows on the bar but now stood up to his full height. He was at least two inches taller than Stone's six-foot frame. Not exactly a major difference but it gave him enough of a height advantage to allow him to look down at Stone with a brazen sneer. "You're that new badass motherfucker of a sheriff, ain't ya?"

"Don't know about badass, but I'm the sheriff, yeah."

"Yeah, I heard about you while I was locked up. Gunned down some survivalists, busted up a meth ring, and took down some neo-Nazi nimrods, right?" Macero snorted. "Yeah, you're a badass son of a bitch, all right. Or at least, you *think* you are." Another snort, this one even more derisive than the first. "Hell, man, I bet my two teenage daughters could take you down. Petra and

Nova know how to scrap. They'd beat your ass for sure."

"Maybe," Stone said. "But they're not here, you are. And it's time for you to go."

"Suck my balls and eat shit, law dog. I ain't going nowhere. After slurping down prison hooch for four years, I came here for some proper booze and I mean to get it."

"And you had it," Stone replied, putting a hard edge on his voice. "Not my fault you can't handle your liquor very well."

Macero's perpetually-squinting eyes narrowed even more, becoming glittering slits. "I hear you right, you cock-sucking cowboy? You just call me a pussy?"

"Didn't call you anything. Just said you're drunk. And because you're drunk, it's time for you to vacate the premises. Easy way or hard way, your choice."

"If by 'easy way' you mean being a sissy bitch and walking outta here just because you told me to, well, then, I guess it's gonna have to be the hard way."

Stone shrugged off his rancher's coat and draped it over the nearest barstool. He could feel the first pulse of adrenaline injecting into his bloodstream, fueling his muscles for the fight. He didn't expect it to be a long one. "Suit yourself," he said. "I'll try not to break any bones, but no promises."

"You'll be lucky if you lay a finger on me."

Macero squared off, rolled his neck through a series of loosening pops, and shifted one foot back in a classic boxer stance, bearing his weight as he brought up his fists. The knuckles looked hard and calloused, either from prison brawls or doing work on a heavy bag. Over on the stage, the guitarist seemed oblivious to the unfolding drama and continued to wail away, providing a screeching soundtrack to the imminent violence.

Stone remained motionless, waiting.

Macero wiggled his fingers in a come-hither motion. "C'mon, cowboy, let's dance."

Stone smiled thinly. "Ladies first."

"Suit yourself."

Macero rushed forward with a bit more skill than Stone had anticipated, dipping and weaving, hands flashing and slashing. But nothing to worry about. Better-than-expected was not the same thing as good-enough-to-get-the-job-done. Stone easily dodged the blows and slammed a short, hard uppercut into the ex-con's chin. Macero's head snapped back and he looked genuinely surprised that he had been hit.

Stone smirked and shrugged. "Guess it must be my lucky day."

Macero shifted his lower jaw back and forth to make sure it still worked, rubbed his bruised chin for a moment, and growled, "Your luck's about to run out."

Stone didn't waste time with a reply. Instead, he fired a short, sharp punch into the man's solar plexus.

The wind wheezed from Macero's lungs and he staggered backward toward the stage where the unaware guitarist kept cranking away on his electric six-string. He had switched to a Bad Company song but the quality had not improved a bit.

Stone followed Macero relentlessly, like a lion stalking prey. He sensed Deputy Sanchez not far behind him but knew she would stay out of the fight. He didn't need help.

Macero lunged forward with a looping haymaker that may have impressed a jailbird on the prison recreation yard but left Stone unfazed. He simply ducked under the punch and drove a hard fist into the man's stomach, doubling him over. He followed up with a rocking uppercut that slammed Macero's mouth shut with the sound of cracking teeth. It was barely audible over the caterwauling guitar but the onlookers winced anyway. Blood bubbled up from cut gums and dribbled over Macero's lips like a drooling red waterfall, spattering on the dirty floor.

Stone seized his advantage. He was trained in all sorts of hand-to-hand combat techniques but he didn't need anything fancy to take down Macero. That being said, the man could definitely take a punch. Stone delivered a rapid-fire series of strikes that should have dumped the ex-con on his backside, but the bastard somehow managed to stay on his feet.

Stone ducked Macero's next punch, grabbed the man's outstretched arm, and executed a powerful throw that jerked him off his feet and sent him skidding across the floor. Macero crashed up against the stage and came to a stop. So did the guitarist, finally realizing there was a fight in progress. The music died with a screech like a rusted buzzsaw.

Macero groaned, as if the pain from Stone's blows was just starting to set in. He glared up at Stone with eyes that were hurting but still brimming with rage.

"Had enough?" Stone asked.

Macero growled a slurred response that was

mostly unintelligible but definitely contained its fair share of four-letter words. He powered to his feet and threw himself at Stone, teeth peeled back from his bloody lips in a feral snarl.

Stone sidestepped the drunken, out-of-control charge and kicked the man's feet out from under him. Momentum threw Macero forward and he landed belly-down with a loud thump, his face bouncing painfully off the floorboards.

The Nailed Coffin was normally loud and rowdy, but right now the place was nearly dead silent, all bleary and bloodshot eyeballs fixed on the fight. Saying you could hear a pin drop would have been an exaggeration, but not much of one. The patrons seemed enthralled to watch Stone dismantle one of their own, perhaps thinking, *There but for the grace of God go I.*

But Stone knew that might not last forever. Mobs are fickle beasts. Best to wrap things up before the crowd decided to come to Macero's aid and turn a one-on-one fight into a full-scale brawl. Stone was in no mood for that much paperwork.

Macero rolled over onto his back, blood seeping from his banged-up nose, and then climbed to his feet again. He swiped the back of his hand across his face, leaving a smear of blood on his cheek like crude war paint.

"Enough of this crap," Stone said. "You took your shot and you lost. Now it's time for you to go."

"Yeah? Go where?" Macero spat a globule of bloody saliva on the floor. "Jail? No fucking way."

"Leave now and I'll let you go home to sleep it off," Stone said. "No harm, no foul, no charges."

"Yeah, right," Macero sneered. "You actually expect me to believe that? I assaulted a cop and you're just gonna let me stroll on outta here."

"Assaulted?" Stone shook his head. "You didn't lay a finger on me."

"Yeah, well, that's about to change."

Macero erupted into violent motion that looked like an amateur martial artist performing a *kata* crossed with drunken break dancing. Somebody in the crowd actually laughed out loud, which sent Macero even further down the rabbit hole of rage. He abruptly abandoned all pretense at karate or kung fu or whatever martial arts hybrid he was trying to exhibit and simply hurled himself forward like the world's skinniest linebacker. He tried to snarl but it came out more like a high-pitched yelp as his arms reached for Stone's waist, aiming to tackle him to the floor.

Stone dodged to the side with ease and clubbed him in the back of the neck, right at the base of the skull, as he stumbled past. It sounded like a hammer smacking a slab of beef. Macero hit the floorboards with his lights out, flopping limply like a rag doll with half the stuffing gone. He wouldn't be getting up for a while. Not without help, anyway. The acrid stench of urine filled the air as the unconscious ex-con abruptly pissed himself.

"You killed him!" someone shouted.

"If I wanted him dead, I could've killed him two minutes ago," Stone rasped. "He's still breathing.

Other than one hell of a hangover and a knot on the back of his head, he'll just be fine."

The barkeeper was shaking his head. "You don't know Vance Macero, Sheriff. The guy's meaner than a junkyard dog with his balls caught in a bear trap, and he don't take a beating well. Believe me when I tell you that this ain't over between the two of you. Ain't over by a long shot."

"Maybe so, but it's over for tonight." Stone turned to Sanchez. "Throw him in a cell to sleep it off and cut him loose when the sun comes up."

The deputy looked concerned and more than a little skeptical. "Your call, sir, but are you sure that's a good idea?"

"No." Stone shrugged on his coat and clamped his Stetson down more firmly on his head. "But I'm going to do it anyway."

FIVE

THE NEXT MORNING ARRIVED CRISP, cool, and utterly calm, not even the hint of a breeze to ruffle what little foliage still clung to the trees. Everything was soaked from last night's storm, dangling raindrops shimmering in the early morning sun, and the sky seemed even bluer than usual, as if grateful to be cleansed of the clouds.

As he drove into town, Stone kept stealing glances toward the high peaks in the distance and wished he was up in those mountains right now, trekking through the brooks and mud and boulders, leaving civilization behind. He longed to cocoon himself in the pungent shadows of the pines and feel the rock ledges beneath his feet. The wild places called to him. Always had and always would. As a preacher, Stone knew you could find God anywhere, but he felt closest to the Creator out in the untamed creation.

He was in town to patch a roof as part of his pastoral duties. Hardly the highlight of his day, but it came with the territory. One of his parishioners, Ralph Richards, owned the furniture store next to the Jack Lumber Bar & Grill. He had called, bright and early—well, actually, it hadn't even been bright yet—to let Stone know that some of his shingles had blown off in the storm and ask if Stone knew anyone who could do the repairs. Richards was a notorious penny pincher—a cheap bastard, most folks called him behind his back, and some right to his face—so what went unspoken in the shop owner's query was that he wanted someone to do it free of charge.

Stone was a mediocre handyman at best, but he volunteered his services. Being a pastor meant serving his congregation and tending to their needs and that didn't mean just their spiritual needs. Christ had said that whatever you did for others was like doing it for Him. No, Richards wasn't poor, he didn't need free labor, but it gave Stone an opportunity to give back. Sometimes his earthly duties as Garrison County sheriff interfered with his spiritual duties as a preacher, and this was one small step toward restoring some semblance of balance between his dual responsibilities. Besides, there was a simple, down-to-earth satisfaction in doing a good deed.

Richards held the ladder steady while Stone climbed up onto the roof with an 80-pound bundle of shingles slung over his shoulder. Truth be told, the manual labor felt good, like he was getting in a workout without having to go to the gym. He made another trip down and up the ladder for his toolbox and then got to work hammering the new shingles in place, driving galvanized nails into the plywood. He found himself concentrating, trying to sink the nails with a single blow.

"How's it look up there, Sheriff?" Richards called out from down below. "Or should I call you preacher today?" His voice dropped to a mutter that still managed to carry up to Stone. "A preacher with a gun. Still the damndest thing I ever heard."

"This patch job will take care of the problem for now," Stone said. "But you're going to need a new roof before too long."

"Costs too much damn money," Richards grumbled. "Hundred-dollar bills don't just grow on trees around here, you know."

"You own a furniture store and drive a brand-new Cadillac," Stone said. "You telling me you can't afford a roof?"

"Maybe I should stop tithing every Sunday and start saving that money."

"That's between you and God." Stone hammered down another nail, this one taking two blows, the sound echoing through the early morning air.

From his aerial vantage point, Stone spotted Tom Benson, the local taxidermist, emerge from the coffee shop up the street. Not the best coffee in town but it got the job done. Benson stood on the sidewalk, looked around, noticed Stone and Richards, and wandered over. He shuffled as much as he walked, his boot soles scraping against the sidewalk.

"Morning, gentlemen." He wore a knit cap and heavy sweater against the autumn chill, the sweater striped in alternating red and green that reminded Stone of Freddy Krueger in *Nightmare on Elm Street*.

Steam from the taxidermist's coffee twisted into the cold air like smoke from the cigarette he fired up, the fragrant scent of tobacco wafting up to where Stone worked on the roof. Stone had never smoked much in his life, but plenty of his warrior buddies had, and he recognized the scent as a Marlboro.

"I see you've got the breakfast of champions going on," Stone called down. "Caffeine and nicotine."

"Match made in heaven." Benson hefted the coffee cup. "But don't worry, it's decaf."

"What about the cigarette?"

"It's not decaf." Benson exhaled a stream of smoke, took a swig of coffee, and then asked, "You fixing the roof?"

"You don't miss much, do you, Tom."

The taxidermist grinned sheepishly. "Yeah, yeah, that was a stupid question." He took another drink of coffee. "Wouldn't you rather be hunting? Maybe shoot a big ol' buck and bring me some business? Order a full shoulder mount and I'll give you the preacher's discount, ten percent off."

Stone thought of the famous Hemingway quote: *There is no hunting like the hunting of man, and those who have hunted armed men long enough and liked it, never care for anything else thereafter.*

Stone knew there were men for whom that held true, but he wasn't one of them. Despite all those years spent as a manhunter, despite all the evil men he had killed, he still enjoyed going out into the woods and hunting wild game. Despite the death and blood that came with dropping a game animal, there was something pure about the sport, a purity that was utterly lacking when putting the crosshairs on a human target.

"I hope to get out in the woods soon," Stone replied. "But it won't be today. As you can see, I'm a little busy."

"Rut will be kicking into high gear pretty soon," Benson said. "You don't want to miss that. Bunch of lovesick bucks running around like their tails are on fire, trying to get some purty little doe to hold still for twenty seconds."

Richards waved an annoyed hand at the taxidermist. "Go away, Tom. Don't you have some Styrofoam to shove up some dead animal's ass or something? Let the preacher work."

Benson ignored him, took another drag on his cigarette, and then tapped away the ash.

"How's your wife doing?" Stone asked.

Benson shrugged. "Well, she's still got cancer." He took the cigarette out of his mouth, stared at it with a *what-the-hell-am-I-doing* look, and then tossed it away as if suddenly disgusted by his bad carcinogenic habit.

"I'll say a prayer for her," Stone said.

Another disheartened shrug. "If the good Lord was listening to prayers these days, preacher, then my Judy wouldn't have cancer anymore." He turned and headed back to his shop, shoulders stooped as if crushed down by an invisible cross. His boots scuffed the sidewalk with an air of dejection and he tossed his coffee in a trashcan as he walked by, looking to all the world like a man who had given up hope.

Stone watched him go, feeling sympathy well up in his chest. At times like this, he almost hated being a preacher. People wanted answers to the hard questions. Questions like, *"Why does a supposedly loving God let people get cancer?"* And the truth was, Stone had no answers to give. Faith was full of mysteries, and that was one of them.

So, instead of trotting out trite, shallow slogans that helped sell bumper stickers at the Christian bookstore but didn't do shit to comfort the hurting, Stone just got back to work. Repairing roofs was a whole lot easier than repairing wounded hearts.

———

Preston Daggett's beloved Golden Retriever, Kingston, was partially paralyzed from the neck down. A pair of herniated discs in the dog's neck had swelled enough to pinch his spinal cord, significantly hampering the movement of his limbs. The poor mutt also suffered from elbow dysplasia, an abnormal growth of cells, tissue, and bones that results in the degeneration of joints.

Surgery for both ailments was available, but the cost was significant and Daggett just didn't have the money. The position of county historian didn't pay much, barely enough to cover the regular household bills, and there simply wasn't enough funds left over to afford expensive surgery for a dog that, at best, only had two or three more years left. People clucked their tongues, shook their heads, and kindly but coldly advised him to *"put the dog down."* Hell, even his wife told him it was time, though Elissa had been less cold than the others.

But Daggett simply could not bring himself to go through with it. He wasn't ready to sit on the cold tile floor of a sterile veterinarian exam room with Kingston's head cradled in his lap while the lethal drugs did their thing. He kept praying for a miracle, kept hoping that he could somehow nurse his best friend back to a painless—or at least less painful—life.

A long shot? Hell yeah, it was. Daggett knew recovery most likely wasn't in the cards, but he refused to give up. He firmly believed that when an animal was ready to die, they found a way to let their owners know. Kingston had not done that. As far as Daggett was concerned, Kingston wasn't ready to cross the rainbow bridge.

The Golden Retriever gave him a warm woof and thumped his tail as Daggett came down the stairs dressed in his camouflage hunting clothes, being as quiet as possible so as to not wake Elissa. He spent a few moments ruffling the dog's ears and then gave him some food and water. By the time he pulled on his boots and headed out the door, Kingston was lying on his favorite dog bed at the end of the couch.

"Be a good boy, Kingston. I'm gonna go get us some venison. That'll make your old bones feel better, hey? Nothing like some good ol' deer liver to put a pep in your step again. I'll tell you all about the hunt when I get back."

The Widow Unser's farm was a hunting paradise, at least for the Adirondacks, located a few miles outside of town on the stretch of road between Whisper Falls and Saranac Lake. The property was a perfect mix of rolling hardwoods and lush agricultural fields that attracted all sorts of game, including deer, bear, and turkey. There was enough acreage to roam around on if you were inclined to spot-and-stalk or still-hunt, but this morning Daggett and Lepper would be plunking their butts down in a couple of the permanent blinds that populated the farm.

Lepper had texted to say he was running late—nothing new for that guy—so Daggett would get on stand first and they would meet up after the morning hunt to share some coffee and tell lies about how many deer they had seen.

Daggett enjoyed deer hunting and studied the sport extensively, subscribing to the usual magazines like *Outdoor Life* and *Field & Stream*, as well as following dozens of hunting-themed pages on social media and YouTube channels. He wouldn't go so far as to call himself an expert, but he was no amateur either, and he had bagged his fair share of big bucks over the years. The antlers adorning the walls of his garage testified to his prowess.

It was still dark when Daggett walked across the field toward his stand, dawn nothing more than a bluish smudged suggestion in the sky. He used a headlamp to navigate the terrain, the light picking up a myriad of deer tracks in the mud along the edge of the field. The soaking rain from last night's storm had churned the earth into a quagmire that sucked at his knee-high rubber boots. So much for making a quiet approach to his stand. Right now, every deer within a quarter mile could hear him trudging through the swampy ground. He might as well have banged some pots and pans together while he was at it.

He pressed on, undeterred. People who waited for perfect conditions to hunt rarely hunted. Adaptation was the name of the game. He would get to his stand long before the sun crested the mountains, and by the time legal shooting light arrived, the woods would have settled back down after his intrusion. With a little luck, a nice buck would fill his crosshairs soon after that and he could head back home to Kingston with fresh meat in the back of his truck and a new set of antlers for his wall.

The pre-dawn darkness was cold, the mid-November air just a degree or two above freezing, but Daggett still mustered up a light sweat by the time he reached his destination. It was one of his favorite spots, an elevated box blind overlooking a small pond that he knew from personal experience was stocked with perch and bullhead. It served as the only natural water source on the whole farm, meaning it was frequently visited by all the wild animals, making it a prime spot to ambush a thirsty buck.

Keeping as quiet as possible, he unloaded his pack, hanging his binoculars, grunt call, and synthetic rattling horns on hooks screwed into the walls of the blind. He wasn't sure if he would actually do any rattling or calling today but he had packed the equipment just in case. Better to have it and not need it than to need it and not have it.

His most important piece of gear right now was the thermos of coffee. Once he had reached the box blind and stopped moving, the sweat had quickly cooled and left him chilled. Time for a liquid warm-up before the sun showed its face and kicked off the morning.

He idly wondered if Lepper would make it to his watch—a ground blind on top of an oak ridge—before sunup, but admitted to himself that he didn't really give a damn. Lepper was a good friend, but right now, they were at odds with each other over the strip club issue, and truth be told, Daggett would rather just hunt by himself. It didn't help that Lepper fancied himself a bit of a know-it-all when it came to deer hunting and constantly prattled on about everything from rifle cartridges to shot placement to field dressing techniques. As if Daggett was some kind of wet-behind-the-ears rookie who didn't know what he was doing and needed someone to hold his hand. Seriously, Lepper's smug, rambling, unsolicited lectures about ballistic coefficients were enough to make a deaf man want to cut off his own ears.

I've got a dozen trophy bucks hanging in my garage, he thought. *All Steve shoots are spikehorns and four-pointers. The only reason he got that six-pointer two years ago was pure dumb luck. But he wants to tell me how to get it done? Screw that noise.*

He sipped coffee and watched the yellow ball of the sun crest the mountains, the darkness giving way to the gray of dawn and then finally the bright blue of the morning. Tendrils of mist rose off the pond water, twisting through the cattails like fleeting ghosts as chickadees flitted in the nearby saplings and trilled their welcome song.

Daggett opened one of the blind's shooting

windows and rested his rifle barrel on the ledge. Three well-trampled game trails cut through the tall grass around the pond, all converging at a point slightly to his left, where the bank dipped down for easy access to the water. As he watched, a fox trotted in, took a furtive drink, and then scurried away. Daggett smiled to himself. Seeing things like that was just one of the many reasons he loved being in the woods.

Off in the distance, he saw smoke rising straight up into the windless sky like a white pillar from the Widow Unser's chimney. He made a mental note to cut her some firewood as a way to say thanks for letting him hunt here. Not everyone who asked was given access to the Widow Unser's land. She was a kind woman but sharp-tongued and would happily tell you to go to hell if she took a disliking to you. Thankfully, Daggett stayed on her good side. He was a little surprised that she tolerated Lepper and would not be surprised if all the controversy about him opening a strip club got him booted off the property next hunting season.

About twenty-five minutes later, the buck appeared.

It came in quiet, not using any of the primary game trails, but slinking through the thick saplings to the right of the blind. It paused a long time before stepping out of the cover and down into the water to drink. It was less than fifty yards from Daggett's position and he could tell it was a monster buck.

He knew the old hunting adage that you shouldn't count the horns until the buck was dead on the ground, but he couldn't help himself. Turned out the whitetail boasted fourteen symmetrical points with a wide spread and lots of antler mass. A trophy buck for sure, maybe even a record breaker.

But first, he had to bag it.

His heart pounded so loud that he expected the deer to hear it and spook. Despite decades of hunting experience, Daggett struggled to control the trembling caused by the adrenaline spiking through his veins. It was like someone had injected *"the shakes"* directly into his bloodstream.

Moving ever so slowly, avoiding any sudden motion that would alert the drinking buck to his presence, Daggett brought the rifle to bear. The Remington Model Seven featured a synthetic stock and stainless-steel barrel chambered in 7mm-.08 with a 4x9 Leupold scope on top. Daggett tucked his eye behind the lens and centered the crosshairs just behind the whitetail's front leg, about halfway down, just above the knuckle. It was the classic kill-shot, taken by thousands of hunters every season. Daggett knew plenty of hunters that aimed for the shoulder or neck, claiming it put the animal down quicker, but he stuck with what had worked for him all these years.

He took a deep breath.

Exhaled, long and slow.

Then squeezed the trigger with slow, steady pressure until the rifle recoiled against his shoulder. Ramped up on adrenaline and excitement, he didn't even feel the gun's kick.

The buck collapsed as if an "off switch" had been flipped. Its legs buckled and it crashed to the ground, part of its body splashing into the water. The sound of the shot reverberated through the woods like a peal of rolling thunder.

Daggett worked the bolt of his rifle up and back to eject the empty cartridge, the brass shell bouncing off the wall of the blind and landing quietly on the carpeted floor. He then threw the bolt forward to chamber a fresh round in case the deer wasn't quite dead. He'd seen plenty of whitetail bucks go down only to bounce back up moments later and go bounding away, leaving an unprepared hunter heartsick and losing hope.

Daggett watched the fallen buck through the scope for a full minute, crosshairs locked on the shoulder, ready to deliver a follow-up shot if necessary. When the deer stayed down and unmoving, Daggett climbed down from the blind and moved cautiously toward the motionless animal. He knew sometimes a rack that looked huge while the buck was alive suffered the so-called "*ground shrinkage*" once the deer was harvested, meaning it was considerably less impressive than it had appeared at first sight. But that was not the case here. The fourteen-point, perfectly symmetrical crown of bone still looked huge, even if the whitetail king that wore it was dead. The early morning sunlight gleamed on the antlers, making them shine. They were mostly a light ivory color but laced with chocolate-brown streaks to give them a unique look.

As he neared the monster buck, Daggett started to truly believe that he might have actually bagged a record-breaker. He had informally scored racks before and with growing excitement, he estimated this one would easily exceed 200 inches. Truly a world-class whitetail, one that might soon be listed among the top ten biggest bucks ever harvested. At the very least, the top fifteen.

Moments later, Daggett leaned his rifle against a nearby pine tree and kneeled down to run his hands over the buck's thick brown coat and white underbelly and then up over the soft, velvety ears. He saw the bullet hole in the buck's boiler room, slightly forward from where he had been aiming. No doubt he had drilled both lungs, but the way the buck had instantly collapsed made him think he had probably busted through some shoulder bone too. He would know more once he got the gutting done.

But before that happened, it was time to brag.

He called Lepper, not really caring if he interrupted his friend's hunt. But it went right to voicemail. No surprise, really. Lepper probably had his cell phone silenced so he wouldn't spook the deer if a call came through.

Daggett left him a message. "Steve, I hope your late and lazy ass is here hunting somewhere, because I'm gonna need help dragging out this beast I shot. Nailed a fourteen-pointer, and it's a smasher. Seriously, man, this is the kind of buck Bass Pro Shops pays good money to put on their wall. You gotta see this monster. Give me a call when you get this."

He hung up the phone, resisting the urge to Google how much money he could get for selling the buck if it turned out to be some kind of new record. Maybe he would be able to get Kingston that surgery after all. He would happily give up the trophy whitetail if it meant a few more years with his four-legged friend.

But first things first, and the first thing was to get this monster field dressed. Would have been a whole lot easier with Lepper's help, but he would manage. Any hunter worth a damn knew how to gut a deer without assistance.

He took out his knife and kneeled down beside the deer, getting ready to use the razor-sharp blade to open the buck up from breastbone to balls.

Better you than me, buddy.

It was his last thought.

SIX

THE ROOF-PATCH JOB FINISHED, Stone was back in his office at Faith Bible Church when Milton Robbins walked in, his six-foot-two, broad-shouldered frame filling the doorway, his salt-and-pepper hair buzzed short, military style.

Robbins had done two tours in Vietnam as a helicopter door-gunner, raining high-velocity hell down on the VC from behind his M60, and was damn proud of his service. He had a box full of medals that he had shown Stone once, with none of the sheepish embarrassment some vets displayed when talking about their accolades. Right now, he held a laptop in his hand.

Robbins had a lean face, large nose above narrow lips, and bushy eyebrows that shielded sunken eyes. Those eyes brimmed with unshed tears as he stared at Stone, not yet saying anything. He had been coming to the church for the past six months, and not once had

Stone seen so much raw, naked emotion on the man's face.

"Everything all right, Milton?" he asked.

The veteran looked uneasy and the laptop in his hand trembled. Not a lot, but enough to be noticeable. "No," he replied. "No, everything is definitely not all right." His face reddened, his uneasiness now colored by shame. "Need to talk to you about something, preacher. About something…well, something embarrassing. Guess you could say I've got a confession to make."

"Well, I'm not a priest, but I'll hear what you have to say and help you work through it." Stone gestured at the chair in front of his desk. "Come on in and have a seat."

Robbins hesitated. His eyes flitted in their sockets and he looked ready to run out the door at any second. "I don't know," he muttered. "I think…I think maybe this was a bad idea."

"Just tell me what's wrong, Milt."

"I don't know if I can, preacher."

"One word after the other, until it's all out," Stone said. "I can't help unless you tell me what's eating you."

Robbins stared at him for several long seconds and then seemed to reach a decision. With a short, sharp nod of his head, he stepped over and set the laptop down on Stone's desk. He then began to pace the room, head down, hands clasped behind his back. He looked like a condemned man waiting to hear what his punishment would be. His lips were pursed together so tight it looked like they might snap at any second.

"You're making me nervous," Stone said.

Robbins snorted. "Bullshit. Nothing makes you nervous, preacher. Sometimes I think you could juggle three rattlesnakes and two chainsaws at the same time and not even break a sweat."

"That's a lie and you know it. Best I could do was two rattlesnakes and one chainsaw."

Robbins smiled, but it was forced, threatening to crumble around the edges like overbaked clay. "You got a way with words, preacher."

"Not my words I'm worried about," Stone replied. "I need you to start using yours and tell me what brought you here."

Robbins glanced at the laptop like it was radioactive and kept on pacing.

"Whatever's got you worked up, I'm not here to judge," Stone said. "I'm here to help."

Robbins stopped pacing, closed his eyes, and took a deep breath. Stone watched and waited. Clearly the veteran was working up the courage to explain the reason for his visit. Stone would let him take all the time he needed. Sometimes the truth didn't like to be rushed.

A few more heartbeats ticked by, and then Robbin's eyes popped open and he blurted out, "I've got a porn addiction." The confession came out so fast that the five words sounded like one.

"All right," Stone said. "I'm not justifying anything here, but that's a pretty common problem for a lot of guys."

"You know a lot of guys that need to jerk off four times a day?" Without waiting for an answer, Robbins gestured at the laptop. "I've got thousands, maybe tens of thousands, of files on that computer. My favorite sites are all bookmarked." He looked miserable and ashamed and there were tears in his eyes. "Go ahead, open it up, see all the sin I've been hoarding."

Stone shook his head. "I don't need to do that."

"There's one site on there called mountainmount dot com. It's a place where Adirondack couples upload their amateur videos."

Stone leaned back in his chair. "Any reason you're telling me about that particular site?"

Robbins shrugged and said, "There are church members on there. Thought you might want to know."

"Actually," Stone replied, "I don't. We've all got our secret sins and unless somebody tells me about theirs, I figure those sins are between them and God."

"No condemnation?" Robbins asked. "No judgment?"

"Judge not lest ye be judged," Stone said. He pointed to the leather-bound Bible on his desk. "Pretty sure I read that in there somewhere."

Robbins nodded. "You're a good man, preacher. Most every other goddamned pastor—uh, sorry, pardon my language—I've ever known would have been all in a lather to go through those files and dig up some names."

"I have no intention of going through those files," Stone said. "But I gotta ask you—is there anything illegal on this computer?"

Robbins furrowed his brow. "What do you mean, illegal?"

Stone gave him a look. "You know. *Illegal.*"

"Oh, God, you mean, like, kiddy stuff?" Robbins appeared nauseous at the thought. "Good Lord, no, preacher. I'm just a porn addict, not a monster."

"Fair enough. What do you want from me?"

"Some counseling, maybe. Your prayers, for sure. Pretty sure the only way I'm gonna get through this is with God's help. And I want you to destroy that laptop."

"Sure, I can do that. Give my sledgehammer a workout."

"I'm really sorry, preacher. I'm so ashamed of myself right now—well, actually, all the time—and I didn't know who else to turn to."

"Happy to help any way I can. You sure you don't want me to just delete the files and give you back the laptop?"

Robbins shook his head emphatically. "No more computers for me. The temptation to look at things I shouldn't be looking at is just too much for me. I want you to smash that thing to hell, where it belongs."

"Probably a good call on your part," Stone replied. "Like Jesus said, 'If your eye offends you, then pluck it out.'"

"Seems a bit drastic," said Robbins. "Then again, if it would make me stop lusting after Elissa Daggett, it might be worth it."

Stone arched his eyebrows. "Elissa Daggett?"

Robbins blushed a shade of red so deep that he practically turned purple. "She actually has a lot of videos on the mountainmount website. She is—she *was*—one of my favorites. There's a whole folder on the laptop dedicated solely to her." He heaved a huge, burdened sigh. "Like I said, preacher, I've got a problem."

"Don't beat yourself up too much," said Stone. "I'm not saying it's right, but lust is natural and men are hardwired wired to look."

"Almost sounds like you're justifying it. Or at least excusing it."

"Not at all," Stone replied. "Just saying that as far as sin goes, lust is one of the harder ones to control."

"I can't stop thinking about the things I've seen, the things I've watched," Robbins said quietly, the shame still dripping from his words like bitter acid. "Those girls...they're somebody's daughter, somebody's sister, somebody's wife. I had no right to look at them." He shook his head. "God forgive me."

"He will," Stone assured him. "All you have to do is ask."

"I know, preacher. But I wanted to let you know about it too, so you can help hold me accountable."

"No problem," Stone replied. "Anytime you feel the devil gunning for you, give me a call."

"And I want you to destroy that laptop. Make it look like one of those thousand-piece puzzle sets."

"I'll take care of it."

They spent a few moments in prayer together and then Robbins departed, still looking guilty and broken. No surprise there, really. Stone knew better than most that faith was not some magic pixie dust that made all your troubles instantly disappear. The road to recovery, to healing, was often long and winding and full of shadows. Good for Robbins for taking his first step down that road, but it would not be his last, and the way would not be easy.

The phone rang, pulling him away from his thoughts. He glanced at the caller ID and saw that it was the station. If they were calling him here at the church, it probably wasn't good news.

He picked up the receiver. "This is Stone."

"Sheriff, it's Valentine." The red-haired deputy sounded urgent.

"What's going on?"

"We've got a body."

"Homicide?"

"No, looks like a freak accident."

"What's the location?"

"The Widow Unser's farm."

"Is it her?"

"No."

"Got an ID?"

"Yeah, we sure do," Valentine said. "It's Preston Daggett."

"I'll be there in ten." Stone hung up the phone, shrugged on his coat, and clamped his

Stetson down on his head.

Knowing he couldn't leave a computer saturated with pornography just laying around the church office —Deacon White would have a field day if he found it —Stone took the laptop with him and tossed it in the back of the Blazer next to a first aid kit.

He had promised to destroy it and he would, but it would have to wait until later. Right now, he had more pressing things to deal with.

Dead bodies trumped naked ones.

SEVEN

LIGHTS AND SIREN BLARING, Stone headed out to the Unser farm. As he raced down Route 3, other vehicles on the road obligingly moved out of his way, pulling over onto the shoulder until he passed them.

Preston Daggett dead? Stone shook his head. It didn't seem real yet and probably wouldn't until he set eyes on the body. He wasn't close to Daggett by any stretch of the imagination but the man was a fixture in Whisper Falls, always happy to chat with anyone who would listen about the history of the town and Garrison County. Despite the altercation at the Jack Lumber last night, Daggett was a fairly gentle, easygoing guy. He deserved better than to die in some random hunting accident. Then again, he had died doing what he loved and Stone reckoned there was some small comfort in that.

He pulled into the Widow Unser's farm and

trekked across the field toward the scene of the accident, following the directions Deputy Valentine had texted him during the drive over. His mood was somber. He had witnessed a lot of death in his time, much of it at his own hand, and while he had become hardened to the sight, he never looked forward to it. There was something unnerving about a corpse, an empty shell with all vitality gone, the spirit drained, the soul departed. Few things forced someone to wrestle with their own mortality faster than coming face to face with the broken husk of the dead.

Stone shook off the grim thoughts as he approached the scene. He saw Deputy Valentine and Deputy Lewis—a.k.a. 'Catfish'—standing by the edge of the pond, near Daggett's body. The Widow Unser hovered nearby, wringing her hands while maintaining a respectful distance, and Steve Lepper slumped on a nearby log, face buried in his hands. His shoulders heaved as he sobbed silently.

As Stone got closer, he saw that Daggett was impaled on the antlers of a giant whitetail buck. It looked like at least two tines had punctured the historian's chest, one directly in the heart.

How the hell…?

"Hey, Sheriff," Valentine greeted, then gestured at the body. "He couldn't have been here too long."

"What makes you say that?"

"He isn't soaked from all that rain last night." Valentine looked damn proud of his detective skills.

"Good observation," Stone said, throwing him a bone. "I saw him last night at the Jack Lumber. Said he was going hunting this morning with him." Stone gestured at Lepper.

"Yeah, he's the one who found the body and called it in." Valentine pushed his hat back on his head and scratched at his fiery red hair. "Ever seen anything like this before?"

"I've seen men killed by animals before," Stone said, "but never a deer." He crouched down on his heels beside the bodies—one animal, one human—and studied them. Blood from the chest wounds had run down the buck's antlers and stained the hair on its head. Stone's earlier assessment that one of the tines had pierced Daggett's heart was correct. Looked like the other one had stabbed into his left lung. If there was a saving grace here, it was that Daggett had died quickly. Maybe not instantly, but he didn't suffer long.

Damn small comfort.

"I can't believe he's dead," the Widow Unser said. "I just spoke with him yesterday."

"Anyone else out here on the property?" Stone asked.

"Not that I know of. Mr. Daggett and Mr. Lepper were the only two people I gave permission to hunt here today. But it wouldn't be the first time someone trespassed onto the farm." She shook her head sadly. "I'll go back to the house and make some coffee and snacks. You and the boys feel free to stop by when you're done here."

"Thanks."

As she moved off, Stone spotted Catfish talking to Lepper. The deputy's usually boisterous voice was quiet and sympathetic. Stone made his way over to the two men and Lepper lifted his head from his hands, tears streaking his face and threatening to freeze on his cheeks in the cold air. "He's dead, Sheriff," he said, stating the obvious in his grief. "My friend...my *best* friend...is dead."

Stone nodded. "Sorry for your loss, Steve."

"I have to tell his wife." Lepper choked back a sob. "Poor Elissa...she's going to be devastated."

"We can break the news to her. You don't have to do it."

Lepper shook his head. "Thanks, but no. It's better she hears it from me."

Stone actually agreed with him. It was the small-town way to have a friend deliver bad news instead of a government official wearing a badge. That might not fly in the big city, but it was the way things were done around here, a taste of old-school America. Locals looking out for locals, friends taking care of friends.

Stone looked at Catfish. "We need to get Daggett off those horns and bagged up. Think you and Valentine can handle that?"

"We'll manage, boss. This ain't my first rodeo and this ain't my first cadaver." He quickly glanced at Lepper. "Sorry if that sounded callous. No disrespect to the dead intended."

Lepper waved away the apology with a weak-wristed gesture, as if he barely had the strength to raise his hand. "No offense taken, deputy."

As Catfish moved away to oversee the gruesome task, Stone sat down on the log next to Lepper. The bark felt cold and rough through the seat of his jeans. "You found the body?"

Lepper sniffled and nodded. "I was running late, so Preston started hunting without me. He left me a voicemail saying he'd bagged a real smasher. When I got here, that's how I found him."

"Looks like a freak accident," Stone said.

Lepper brushed away a fresh tear. "You hunt, Sheriff?"

"When I have the time."

"Then you already know what happened here. Preston didn't make sure the buck was dead when he approached. Probably was so excited to wrap his hands around those beautiful horns, and when he did, the buck gored him to death."

"That'd be my guess, too," Stone agreed.

"What really sucks is that he knew better," Lepper said. "Every hunter worth his salt knows that you need to make sure the deer is dead before you get close. Personally, I always poke it in the eye with my rifle barrel. If it's alive, it'll blink every time. No blink, you know you're good to go."

"I do the same thing," Stone replied. "Like you say, if that buck is still alive when you stick a gun barrel in its eye, it's gonna flinch."

Lepper shook his head and glanced over to where the two deputies were pulling the body off the deer's antlers. He winced at the wet sucking sounds as the bloody tines pulled free of the chest wounds. "I can't believe Preston shot a world-class buck and it got him killed. Of all the rotten luck..." His eyes shifted to Stone. "How long before you can release his body? I'm sure Elissa will want to make his funeral arrangements as soon as possible."

"Shouldn't take too long," Stone said. "I'll have the coroner put a rush on the autopsy."

"Autopsy?"

Stone nodded. "Pretty standard procedure in accidental deaths."

"Not sure Elissa is going to like that."

"I'll get the body released to her as fast as I can."

"Thanks. I appreciate that, and I'm sure Elissa will too." He pointed at the dead deer. "What's gonna happen to the buck?"

"You want it?"

"Preston died for that buck, and it's a real beauty that's gonna break some records. I'd like to get it mounted and make sure Preston gets the recognition that he deserves in the hunting community. It's the least I can do to honor his memory."

"I'll let you tag it on one condition," Stone said.

"What's that?"

"You don't hang the head in your strip club." Stone smiled slightly. "I don't think Daggett would have appreciated that."

Lepper chuckled, though it was laced with sadness. "You're right about that. I think the old bastard would come back from the grave and haunt me."

Stone stood up from the log and brushed off his pants as Valentine and Catfish zipped up the body bag holding Preston Daggett's earthly remains. "No way to get a vehicle back here," Valentine said. "Woods are too thick. We'll have to carry him out."

"Get him back to the farmhouse and then call the coroner for a transport," Stone said.

Lepper turned his head away, looking off at the mountains in the distance, some of the peaks already capped with high-elevation snow. "I can't believe he's gone," he murmured, talking more to himself than anyone else.

Stone put a comforting hand on the man's shoulder. "We'll take care of him. Why don't you go home, find Elissa, and give her the news. I may have a few more routine questions down the road for my report, but they can wait."

"Thanks, Sheriff." Lepper sighed heavily and stood up. "Telling Elissa is going to be one of the hardest things I've ever done. Real damn hard. She's a strong woman, but she's not going to handle this well."

"Losing someone you love is one of the hardest things in this life to go through," Stone said, thinking of his daughter buried under six feet of Texas dirt. "If there's anything I can do for you or Elissa, let me know."

Lepper nodded, gave Stone a weak smile, and then walked away. His shoulders slumped as he made his way through the trees, heading back to the farm. Off in the distance, a crow cawed, like some kind of death harbinger announcing Daggett's passing.

Stone watched Lepper go and felt sympathy for the man. He knew all too well what the weight of grief felt like. He thought of his daughter again and this time felt the sting of tears behind his eyes, even after all these years. Time heals all wounds? Yeah, that was a damned lie. Time lessened the pain enough to let you go on living, but the wound remained. Lepper had just lost his best friend, and that kind of pain stuck with you for the rest of your life.

Stone turned and looked down at the giant buck. It was a magnificent beast, a genuine monster, and he had no doubt it was going to break some records.

Too bad it had broken some hearts in the process.

EIGHT

HIDING out inside the locker room, Lizzy heard the shouts of the girls playing in the gymnasium. Volley-ball, judging from the sounds. She wondered how long it would take for anyone to notice she was skip-ping gym class. With luck, no one would pay any attention to her absence. She didn't feel like dealing with life right now, and that included the banalities of Phys Ed. She would just sit here on the bench between lockers, scroll through videos on her phone, and try to forget her troubles.

That worked perfectly fine until her troubles walked in.

The fucking Macero twins.

Nova and Petra.

They weren't identical twins but pretty damn close. Both had black, slightly curly hair that hung midway down their backs, sometimes loose, usually in pony-tails. Their faces were long and oval-shaped, with thin-bladed noses and cruelly twisted mouths set beneath dark, glinting eyes. Their ears were heavily pierced, each sporting a half-dozen holes, and Petra wore a nose stud in her left nostril.

Somewhere around seventh grade, they had adopted an air of perpetual disdain for those they judged beneath them, and these days, that was Lizzy. They cared nothing about grades, the social hierarchy of high school, or pretty much anything other than making her life miserable. As far as Lizzy knew, she had not done anything to piss them off, but they had made her a target for their bullying cruelty anyway. One of those random things, just another example of life taking a big, giant crap on her head. You would think she'd be used to it by now.

The twins' heads swiveled on their necks as they looked around to make sure they were alone, and then they sauntered over to Lizzy, rubbing their hands together like witches excited about cooking children in a cauldron.

No, not witches, Lizzy reminded herself. *Bitches*.

"Hey, Liz-bo, what're you doing hiding in here all by yourself?" Nova asked in a mocking, sing-song tone while her sister giggled encouragement. Nova was chewing gum and snapped a bubble as if it was the coolest thing ever. "Hiding from the world? Thinking about killing yourself? God, it would be so great if you did. Go ahead, get it done, girl. Believe me, nobody will miss your sorry ass. Hell, I think I've even got a razor blade in my backpack you can use. Just rip them veins wide open, and we'll keep you company while you bleed out."

Lizzy just stared at them, eyes hot and angry. They

wanted a response, *craved* a response, and so she refused to give them the satisfaction. But in her head, she was wondering if she could gouge out their eyes and get away with it.

Petra snatched the cell phone from Lizzy's grasp with the unexpected speed of a magician performing a sleight-of-hand trick. She began scrolling through the phone's content, her face contorted into a mockery of exaggerated enthrallment.

"Give it back," Lizzy snapped. "Now."

"What's the matter, Liz-bo?" Nova said. "Afraid we might find something you don't want us to see?"

"I'm gonna find some nudes and send them to all the guys in school," Petra taunted. "By this time tomorrow, everybody will know what your itty-bitty-titties look like."

"I said, give it back." Lizzy injected venom into her voice as she reached out to take the phone away from Petra.

Petra shoved her away. "Keep your filthy hands to yourself, bitch."

"Finding anything good on there?" Nova asked her sister.

Lizzy lunged off the bench, ready to make another attempt to reclaim her phone, but stepped on Nova's foot in the process.

"Watch where you're going, you dumb slut!" Without warning, Nova hauled back her fist and slugged Lizzy in the nose.

Stunned, Lizzy stumbled back until she hit the wall, her elbow banging off the side of a locker. She put her hand up to her face, gingerly checking the damage. Her nose didn't feel broken, but it hurt like hell and blood streamed from her nostrils, running hot and thick over her fingers.

Without really thinking about the potential consequences of her actions, she flicked her hand at Nova, spattering blood all over the girl's blouse. "Fuck you and fuck your sister. And by the way, you hit like a little girl."

Nova stared down at the red polka dot pattern staining her shirt and her face turned an even deeper shade of crimson. "You ruined my blouse, you stupid bitch! It was a birthday present from my grandma!"

"I'll bet she's real proud of the woman you've become," Lizzy said.

With a snarl of rage, Nova grabbed Lizzy, threw her down on the floor, and began kicking her in the stomach. Lizzy curled into a ball and tried to roll away but Petra joined in the beatdown, driving a foot into her kidneys.

Through a blur of pain, Lizzy heard somebody staying stop, over and over again. It took her a moment to realize the words were coming from her own mouth, desperate pleas for the assault to end.

"Please...stop...please..."

She despised the whimpering weakness she heard in her voice but couldn't help it. All she wanted was for this to be over.

Nova kicked her a few more times, then spat her wad of bubblegum out on her. Lizzy felt it bounce off her shoulder and stick in her hair. The twins stood over her like a pair of conquering barbarians surveying their vanquished foe. Blood from her battered nose drooled out onto the floor. Her ribs and stomach hurt so bad that she wondered if she would need to go to the hospital.

"You get the message, you uppity bitch?" Petra asked, dropping the cell phone on the floor in the spattered blood. "Don't mess with us or we'll bring the pain."

"I didn't mess with you," Lizzy said, wincing. "You just get off on hurting people."

Another kick thudded into her thigh, hard enough that she was pretty sure the bruise would go all the way to the bone.

"That smart mouth of yours ain't doing you any favors," Petra said.

Lizzy almost said, *At least I've got something smart on me, unlike you two,* but then decided to keep quiet and spare herself further pain. Wasn't there a quote about silence being the better part of valor, or something like that?

"I can't believe you hit her in the face," Petra said to Nova, her tone scolding.

"The goody-two-shoes dick guzzler deserved it," Nova retorted. "Besides, what do you care? You feeling sorry for her or something now?"

"Hardly." Petra looked disgusted at the thought. "But remember what dad taught us? Hit 'em where it won't show. Not the face."

"Whatever." Nova grabbed a dirty sports jersey hanging on a nearby hook and threw it at Lizzy. "There, use that stinking thing to clean yourself up before you go back to class. Breathe a word about this to anybody and next time we'll stomp you so hard, your guts will come out your asshole."

Lizzy swiped away the blood leaking from her bashed nostrils and tried to ignore the pain flooding through her bruised body as she watched the Macero twins leave the locker room, high-fiving each other and cackling at their latest handiwork.

It wasn't their first time doing this to her, and it wouldn't be the last.

Not unless she did something about it.

Lizzy climbed up off the floor and crawled back onto the bench, slumping against the locker as tears streamed down her face. She wept, but it wasn't from fear or pain.

No, she wept with rage.

I'm going to kill those bitches.

NINE

STONE SPENT the rest of the morning dealing with the paperwork associated with Daggett's accidental death. He despised this part of the job—he was a man of action, not pencil-pushing—but recognized the reports as a necessary evil. The bureaucratic machine needed to be fed, and paper was its preferred sustenance.

Shortly after noon, he left the station, crossed over Wildflower Avenue onto Main Street, and walked a half-block to the Jack Lumber Bar & Grill. The cold air on his face worked like a slap, jolting him out of the lethargy that came from staring at a computer screen too long. His stomach growled, demanding food, and he looked forward to a greasy smash-burger—hold the onions and pickles—and some homemade, generously salted french fries.

There were only a few other customers in the joint, all seated at the booths along the wall, eating their lunches and engaged in conversation. The jukebox cranked out a Def Leppard tune. Stone headed directly to the bar and slid onto a stool as Grizzle made his way over.

"Taking a break from dealing with dead hunters?" the barkeep asked.

"Guess you heard about who got killed out at the Unser farm," Stone said.

Grizzle nodded. "You know how small-town gossip goes. Not much happens around these parts that I don't hear about." He sighed. "Real damn shame, that's what it is. I liked Preston. He was a good man."

"I didn't know him well, but he seemed all right," Stone said. "Certainly didn't deserve what he got."

"Is it true what they're saying? That he got gored to death by a deer?"

"Looks that way. Have to wait for the coroner to confirm it."

"Hell of a way to bite the dust." Grizzle jerked a thumb over his shoulder at the liquor bottles stacked on the shelves behind him. "You want your usual?"

Stone shook his head. "I'm on duty."

"Okay, then," the barkeep said. "One Jack and Coke coming up, lots of ice, hold the Jack."

When Grizzle set the glass down in front of him, the ice cubes rattled against the rim and the carbonation in the cola fizzled and popped. Stone immediately took a drink and let out an appreciative sigh. "You know, for a booze-slinger, you pour a pretty mean Coke."

"Better than the fountain Cokes over at McDonald's everyone's always raving about these days?"

"Let's not get carried away."

"You know, for a preacher, you can be a real asshole," Grizzle said with a grin.

"I'm just saying that a man's got to know his limitations."

"Pretty sure I've heard that somewhere before."

"If you haven't, you have shit taste in movies."

"No, just shit taste in friends."

"If I had feelings, they'd be hurt right now."

"Guess it's a good thing that you're an ice-cold son of a bitch, then." Grizzle winked. "Except when Holly's around, that is. Then you turn into a puppy dog."

"Shut up, Griz."

The bartender laughed and held up his hands in a gesture of surrender. "Suit yourself, padre. But running from the truth ain't a good look for a preacher."

"Maybe you didn't hear me the first time," Stone said, giving him a crooked grin. "Shut up."

"Now that ain't gonna happen and you know it, but I will ease off the Holly thing—for now—and go back to talking about Preston Daggett, may the good Lord rest his soul."

"Such a freak accident." Stone shook his head. "Hard way to go."

Grizzle eyeballed him. "Unless I'm mistaken—and I'm usually not—I'm picking up something in your tone that tells me maybe something ain't sitting right with you."

Stone shrugged. "Nothing I can put a finger on.

Just an itch telling me that maybe I don't know the whole story."

"You got a reason to think it wasn't just an accident?"

Stone shook his head. "Like I said, just sort of an itch I'm feeling."

"Yeah, well, the best thing you can do for an itch is scratch it." Grizzle used the rag that was perpetually draped over his shoulder to wipe away a drop of condensation that ran down Stone's glass and onto the bar.

"Not always," Stone said. "Sometimes scratching an itch does more damage than just leaving it the hell alone."

Grizzle snorted dismissively. "That's what they make ointment for."

"Just because you slap ointment on it doesn't mean there won't be a scar."

Grizzle arched an eyebrow. "Look at you…sheriff, preacher, and now philosopher."

You forgot to add "killer" to that list, Stone thought. He sometimes wondered what Grizzle would think if he told him about his vigilante methods of dispensing justice, but he never actually did it. He suspected the old bartender wouldn't care that much, might even tacitly approve. But there was no reason to find out. That dark side of his nature, his periodic return to his warrior ways, was between him and God.

Stone shrugged. "What can I say? I'm a man of many talents."

"Be careful. You know what they say—jack-of-all-trades, master of none."

"True."

"Think Lepper could've killed him?" Grizzle asked. "Daggett was pretty cranked up about Lepper opening that strip club."

"I don't see it," Stone said. "Lepper seemed genuinely broken up about Daggett's death."

"So we just got some random killer running around out there in the woods like Jason Voorhees, tossing people onto dead buck antlers?"

"Don't go starting that rumor. That's the last thing I need. Just because I got a little itch that something is off about this case doesn't mean there actually is. It's just a freak hunting accident until something proves otherwise."

"Sometimes you gotta trust your gut, Luke."

"We'll see what the coroner says."

"Sounds like a plan." Grizzle drew himself a beer from the tap and raised his glass. "To Preston, a good man taken too soon. May he rest in peace."

Stone raised his glass as well. "To Preston."

The two men remained quiet for several moments following the solemn toast, the deceased's name hanging in the air like smoke.

Their respects paid, Stone ordered his burger. It came medium-rare, just the way he liked it, and he was just munching down the last bite when his cell phone rang. He used a napkin to wipe the grease from his lips, glanced at the caller ID, and saw that it was Holly.

He answered with a smile. "If you're calling to ask me to lunch, you're too—" He stopped talking as Holly's panicked voice filled his ear, dispensing heart-seizing information at a rapid-fire rate that made it impossible to fully decipher what she was saying. But he got the gist of it, and that was enough to make his blood turn cold.

"I'm on my way," he said and hung up.

Grizzle caught the alarmed tone. "Who was that? What's wrong?"

"Holly," Stone replied, throwing on his coat. "Bad news. Gotta go." He reached for his wallet to settle his tab.

Grizzle waved him away. "Your money's no good right now. It's on the house."

"You're a good man, Griz."

"Just don't tell anyone. Now get outta here."

"Thanks."

Less than two minutes later, he was in the Blazer, tires screaming in protest as he punched the gas. He left twin strips of smoking black rubber in his wake as he raced toward Holly's house with lights flashing and siren wailing.

TEN

"JACK—MY EX-HUSBAND—ESCAPED PRISON." Holly stopped pacing back and forth in her living room and looked at Stone with desperate, red-rimmed eyes. "Luke, this is my absolute worst nightmare."

She grabbed a glass of wine off the coffee table and guzzled it down. It was her second glass since Stone had got here six minutes ago. Her Springfield XDS 9mm lay on the table next to a half-empty bottle. Stone knew that the compact pistol would not be out of arm's reach until the situation resolved itself.

He also knew she was perfectly capable of using it if that's what it took to protect herself and Lizzy. She had demonstrated her willingness to kill in self-defense on at least two previous occasions. The murderous survivalist who had targeted her shortly after Stone came to town received two to the chest and one to the head for his trouble. And the drug baroness who had kidnapped Lizzy last year and nearly burned her alive had received a blade in the eye—*both* eyes—for daring to cross that line.

Stone almost asked her for the details of the escape —how the hell did a mob boss break out of a maximum security prison?—but then decided it didn't matter right now. He could always make some calls later if he really wanted to know. What *did* matter was that Jack "Lucky Draw" Dawson was on the loose and very likely on the hunt for the ex-wife who had put him behind bars and the daughter he had tried to abuse.

"I knew this day would come," Holly said, pacing again. "I knew this would happen."

"We'll get through it," Stone said, trying to be reassuring.

"It's not your problem."

"The hell it isn't."

"Luke, he's a very dangerous man."

"What do you think I am?"

She stopped pacing and stared at him. "Sometimes I'm still trying to figure that out."

"What I am is a man who will stop at nothing to protect the people I care about, and Holly, there's nobody on this planet I care about more than you and Lizzy." The warmth of his words abruptly switched to a much harder tone. "So if your scumbag of an ex-husband shows up with intent to do you harm, I'll put him down like a broke dick dog and go to bed that night with a clear conscience."

Holly smiled. "You're a good man, Luke. That much I know."

If you knew everything, you might not think that, Stone thought. Aloud, he said, "Your WITSEC handler said Jack doesn't know where you're located, right?"

"He said there's no way Jack can know and told me to relax." She laughed, the sound harsh and brittle. "Relax? Yeah, right. That's not going to happen. All I want to do is curl up in a ball and cry."

"Understandable, but probably not the best course of action."

"'There's nothing to worry about,' that's what he told me. Can you believe that?" Holly poured herself some more wine, filling the glass right up to the brim. "I mean, why would I worry? My psychotic mobster of an ex-husband, who has vowed vengeance since the day I testified against him, has just escaped from prison. Nothing to worry about, right?"

"He doesn't know your new name or where you live," Stone reminded her. "I'm not going to lie and say he can never find you, but it damn sure won't be easy."

"I know." She went over and stood by the window, staring out into space. "It's been ten years, but I remember it like it was yesterday. Sitting in that hideous motel room with the US Marshals while they gave me my new identity."

Stone watched her, wondering what she was thinking, realizing part of her mind had reverted to the past.

"Your new name is Bennett," Cade Rogers, *her assigned marshal, had informed her. "Holly Bennett."*

"That's ridiculous," she replied. "That's the best you

guys could come up with? Do I look like someone named after a Christmas plant?"

"If I'm being honest..." Marshal Rogers looked her up and down, not lasciviously, but with sympathy in his eyes. "...what you look like right now is a total mess."

"Thanks. You're a real sweetheart." She pulled the thin motel blanket closer around her shoulders like a shawl, wondering why it vaguely smelled like cat piss. But at least it was warm. For the last few days, she had felt chilled to the bone, cold right down to the marrow, hiding out in this tiny, low-budget hotel room with her daughter while the marshals did their thing. Of course, she had done her thing, too. Namely, ratted out her husband, one of the most powerful mob bosses on the west coast. But that's what the bastard got for daring to put his hands on their little girl. She might be afraid, knowing there would be a target on her back for the rest of her life, but she regretted nothing.

Rogers sat down on the bed next to her and patted her hand in a kind, fatherly gesture. There was nothing sexual about it. As guys went, he was definitely no hot stud muffin. He wasn't much taller than she was and he looked more like a bank teller or CPA than a US Marshal. Not somebody she would have chosen to keep her and her daughter—now named Eliza, apparently—safe from the mob, but it wasn't like she had any say in the matter. In her mind, marshals were supposed to be tall, athletic, steely-eyed, with a pistol strapped under their arm. Not short, roundish, wearing glasses, with a cell phone holder clipped to his belt. As first impressions went, Rogers didn't exactly make her feel safe. She'd been tempted to call the whole thing off right then and there.

But what Rogers lacked in physical appearance, he more than made up for with professional competence. It had taken a couple of days, but she learned to trust him.

"Holly, there's nothing to worry about," he said.

She just stared at him, wanting to believe his words but not knowing if she could. She felt lost, adrift, and wondered if she would ever feel safe again.

"Holly?"

A finger-snap in front of her face jerked her from the reverie of her past and brought her back to the present. She turned away from the window and saw Stone standing beside her, watching her closely.

"Holly?" he said again. "Are you all right?"

"I'm fine." She was clearly lying and tried to cover it up by taking a sip of wine. Well, not really a sip, more like a three-chug guzzle.

"You've never slipped up, right? Never contacted anyone from your past, told them where you are?"

"Of course not. I'm not an idiot, Luke."

"Just asking."

"And I'm just answering. Believe me, I've done everything by the book."

"What about Lizzy?"

"What about her?"

"You said she's been acting different lately. Any chance she did something stupid and that's why she's acting that way?"

Holly shook her head. "She was too young to even remember anyone from those old days, let alone reach out to them. Hell, I'm not even sure she remembers what her father tried to do to her." She rubbed her temple as if trying to ward off the onset of a migraine and resumed pacing. "I should have known this wasn't going to work. Upstate New York? Really? I'd never been farther east than St. Louis. I was a Vegas girl, used to life in the big city. Why the hell did they put me up here in the middle of nowhere? If Jack does track me down here, it won't be hard to find me. Kind of hard to disappear into the crowd in a small town."

Stone didn't bother saying that moving her from the west coast to the east coast was the marshals' way of protecting her and Lizzy from her ex-husband. Relocation to the other side of the country was fairly standard operating procedure. He didn't say it because Holly already knew it. But stress and worry were causing her to conjure up unfounded fears.

Instead, he said, "I understand this is news you hoped you'd never hear, but I really wouldn't sweat it too much."

"How can you say that? My ex-husband, who wants me dead, just broke out of prison."

"Maybe he doesn't care about killing you anymore," Stone said. "He's been behind bars for a long time. Now that he's out, he may just want to disappear. Hell, he could be in some non-extradition country like Venezuela by now."

Holly shook her head, a tremor running through her body. "You don't know him, Luke. The man is practically the devil incarnate. I put him in prison and took his daughter away from him. He's not going to just let that go."

"Even if that's the case, he doesn't know where you and Lizzy are."

"Lizzy…" She murmured the name as she slumped down on the sofa, careful not to spill her wine. She looked pale, panicked, fragile.

"What about her?"

She stared up at him with frightened eyes. "Do I tell her that her father is coming for us?"

ELEVEN

LEONARD HOFFMAN'S bleary eyes flickered open as a ray of sunlight penetrated the room through a crack in the shade and lit up his face like a laser beam. He turned away with a groan, pressing his head deeper into the drool-stained pillow.

As he slowly stirred from his stupor, he realized that he was naked, and so was the strange woman in his bed. He blinked, trying to remember how things had played out last night. Judging from his skull-banger of a headache and the pretty young thing lying next to him, he had gotten drunk and managed to score.

Carve another notch on the bedpost for another satisfied customer.

Then again, maybe he had suffered from whiskey dick and passed out, leaving her unfulfilled and unimpressed. Wouldn't be the first time, wouldn't be the last. Sometimes the Viagra helped, sometimes he might as well have taken a multivitamin. And honestly, he didn't really care all that much.

He stared at the woman who was still asleep, body curled into a comma, facing away from him. He struggled to remember her name. Julie? Janice? No, Jennifer. He was sure of it. Her last name didn't matter. Nobody cared about last names during hump-'em-and-dump-'em one-night stands. Actually, nobody cared about first names either when you got right down to it.

Hoffman sat up in bed, moving slowly, his brain a fog. The girl, Jennifer, stirred a little, made a cute little mewling noise, but didn't wake up. He rubbed his temples, willing memory back into his mind. He remembered having a bad week, wanting to relieve some tension, and going out to hunt for some horizontal action. Clearly, he had succeeded, and had not lowered his standards in the process. Jennifer looked nice and young and very fit, just the way he liked them. He much preferred to bang women out of his league. But then, what guy didn't?

Hoffman was well aware of his shortcomings. He was just a shade over five and a half feet tall and going pudgy around the middle like all government desk jockeys eventually did after decades of eating office donuts every morning. His hair had avoided going gray, but only because it had started to fall out instead, leaving him afflicted with the typical male pattern baldness. But he had good cheekbones and hazel eyes that the ladies seemed to like. Or at least, that's what he told himself. And if flashing those eyes didn't work, he could usually flash his federal law enforcement officer credentials and convince some badge bunny to bounce into his bed. Maybe not the sober ones, but hey, did it really matter?

Scraps of memory from last night started to come back to him, but it was mostly just a dark blur streaked with pulsing neon. He remembered a dance club—not his usual hunting ground, but apparently it had worked out just fine—and gyrating with Jennifer while she wore painted-on jeans and a black tank top that exposed a generous amount of cleavage. He vaguely recalled not caring for the way one side of her head was shaved close, but that was hardly a deal breaker, especially when that head was bobbing up and down in his lap.

Hoffman found his boxers on the floor and slipped them on. He briefly considered pouncing on Jennifer and demanding a morning quickie before he kicked her to the curb, but then he decided to be a gentleman today and wait to see if she was actually interested in another round before they said their awkward good-byes and pretended they were actually going to see each other again.

He crept into the kitchen, the tile cold under his bare feet. *Should have put on some slippers, you idiot*, he scolded himself. *Or installed in-floor radiant heat*. He started a pot of coffee and watched impatiently while it dripped itself into caffeinated existence. When it was done, he filled a mug emblazoned with the slogan *I Can't Fix Stupid But I Can Cuff It*. He raised the cup to his lips and slurped appreciatively, eyes closed as he savored the hot beverage.

Over on the counter, his cell phone rang loudly and

vibrated at the same time. He jumped, nearly spilling coffee down his bare chest. He grabbed the phone on the third ring, wondering—but not really caring—if it had awakened his sleepover guest. "Hello?"

"Hoffman? It's Carol Bryant, from the South Central Regional Office. We had an eight o'clock Zoom meeting this morning to review those six cases we discussed last week."

"Are you sure? I thought that wasn't until Thursday."

Bryant cleared her throat. "Uh, today *is* Thursday."

Damn it, Hoffman, get your shit together. He glanced at the LED clock on the stove and saw that it was 8:37. "Sorry about that," he said. "I've been sick and lost track of the days. You know how it goes. We'll need to reschedule our meeting."

"Uh…okay…sure. Can we do it tomorrow, same time?"

"Let me check my schedule and call you back." He didn't wait for confirmation. Just hung up the phone and headed for the bathroom, moving quickly. He needed to haul his ass to work before he missed anymore meetings. Complaints wouldn't look good in his personnel file.

He took a three-minute shower, threw on some navy blue 511 tactical pants and an olive-green polo shirt—the Federal Bureau of Prison's idea of casual business attire—and gave his teeth a ten-second brushing, making sure he scrubbed the film off his tongue. His guts felt sour and he fought back the bile that wanted to rise by promising his stomach to get it some food ASAP.

He laced up his boots and shrugged into his jacket before he remembered the girl in his bed.

Jennifer.

Shit.

He put a hand up to his mouth and made a muffled coughing noise. "Uh, good morning. Listen, I need to hit the road, so…"

Nothing.

"I made coffee. I'm sure you could use some, if your head feels anything like mine."

She threw back the covers and stared up at him, just lying there naked, her pale skin on full display. Hoffman saw the same fog of confusion on her face that he had experienced upon awakening as she clawed her way back toward cognizance. It made her look cute, vulnerable, and made him want to forget about going to work so he could jump back in bed and have another tumble. He felt his body start to respond at the thought.

She slowly rolled out of bed with a long, drawn-out groan. He watched her until he felt like a creep and then looked away. "I have some aspirin or ibuprofen if you need any," he said. "Or Excedrin, if you prefer."

"Any of them will work. Some coffee too, please."

He fetched her a cup along with three ibuprofens. She washed the pills down with a swig of java and immediately gagged. "My God, you call that coffee? Tastes like a cup of mud that a cow pissed in."

"Sorry, Jennifer."

Her eyebrows shot up. "Seriously?" She shook her head in disbelief. "It's Jessica, you dick."

"Sorry about that, too." Hoffman's morning lust retreated, realizing that getting her name wrong had nixed any chances at another romp between the sheets. Now he just wanted her to get her perky little backside moving so he could get to work before it got any later. "Listen, I can drop you off somewhere on the way to the office, but we really need to get going."

"Can I use the bathroom first at least? Jeez, Denny."

"It's Lenny. Well, Leonard, actually."

"Whatever. Just leave, go do whatever you gotta do. I'll take a shower and call an Uber." She headed toward the bathroom, mumbling, "I really need to stop drinking and going home with losers."

Leonard looked at his phone while she showered. He couldn't just leave some woman he barely knew alone in his house. He tried to distract himself with justified homicide videos on YouTube, but the reminders kept popping up on the screen, alerting him to all the unanswered emails and texts he needed to deal with when he eventually dragged his hurting carcass into the office.

When Jessica emerged from the bathroom in a roiling cloud of steam, wearing nothing but her birthday suit, she asked, "What did you say you did? A cop or something?"

"I'm a federal law enforcement officer," Hoffman replied, not even trying to conceal the pride in his voice. "I work for the Department of Justice."

"Doing what?"

"I'm the Assistant Director of the Correctional Programs Division for the Federal Bureau of Prisons."

"Wow, that sounds fancy." Her tone belied her words, making it clear she wasn't impressed. "I thought you were, like, a real cop or something." She slid on her jeans and jammed her feet into her shoes while she used her fingers to comb out her still-damp hair.

"We *are* real…" Hoffman let his voice trail off and shook his head. This little trollop wasn't worth the argument. It wasn't the first time he'd heard that people working for the BOP weren't real officers, and it wouldn't be the last. Of course, the morons who spouted that nonsense wouldn't last ten minutes walking a beat behind the razor wire without shitting themselves. "Forget it," he said. "Just get out of here, will you? I've got places to be."

She shot him the finger as she left the bedroom and headed for the front door. He gave her a vague goodbye gesture, mumbled some lie about calling her later, and looked down at his phone as three more alerts beeped for his attention. God, he was going to be buried in work today.

He heard the front door open, the top hinge creaking loudly to announce its need for oil. A moment later came the low murmur of voices. He looked up from his phone in puzzlement as Jessica called out, "There's some guy here to see you."

Hoffman's hackles went up. *What the hell?* He wasn't expecting anyone, especially not this early in the morning. The feeling that flooded his guts wasn't exactly fear, more like nervous tension. He told himself to relax. Nobody came gunning for a mid-level BOP desk jockey.

He exited the bedroom to see an olive-skinned man with one green eye standing in the doorway, the other socket covered by a black eye patch. As soon as the stranger spotted Hoffman, he slammed his left hand into Jessica's chest and shoved her backward. At the same time, his right hand came up holding a pistol that Hoffman recognized as some kind of Beretta with a suppressor on it.

Jessica stumbled backward with a startled, "Hey!" She tripped over her own feet and turned to Hoffman with a confused look on her face.

The look vanished when the stranger double-tapped her in the back of the head, the exiting bullets turning her features into a gruesome crater of mangled pulp and splintered bone. Hoffman flinched as brains and blood spattered his shirt, creating an abstract pattern of chunky red polka dots.

"What the fuck?" he yelled.

The one-eyed man bulled through the doorway and stalked toward Hoffman, stepping over the fresh-killed corpse. Hoffman thought about making a dash for the gun he kept in a biometric safe in his night-stand drawer but quickly discarded the idea. He would never make it, never get it open in time. Whatever he was about to face, he would have to face it without a weapon.

The intruder squinted, his visible eye narrowing. The black patch he wore looked brand new. "Sorry for the intrusion," he said, not sounding the least bit sorry at all. "Are you Leonard Hoffman?"

"Yeah, I'm Hoffman. Who the fuck are you?"

"I'm Jack Dawson."

"Who?"

"Don't play dumb, Lenny. I broke out of a federal prison two days ago and you work for the Federal Bureau of Prisons, so acting like you don't know my name makes you look like an idiot and insults my intelligence."

Three more men filed into the house and spread out behind Dawson. They were all armed, Hoffman noted, with the same kind of pistol as Dawson.

Must have been BOGO day on Berettas, he thought, followed by, *Shit, I'm in trouble.*

"Fine," he said. "I know who you are. Happy? But what I don't know is why the fuck you're here and what the fuck you want from me."

"We'll get to that in a second," Dawson said. "But first, I want you to think long and hard about whether you want to do things the easy way or the hard way."

"How can I decide that if I don't know what you want?"

"I want the name of the WITSEC handler assigned to my ex-wife."

"I don't have access to that information." The lie rolled off his tongue easily.

"Yes, you do. It's part of my case file, and you have access to the case files of all the prisoners in the federal prison system."

"Even if that was true," Hoffman said, "it would take security clearance above my level to access." At this point, there was no reason not to double down on the lies.

"You oversee the entire Central Inmate Monitoring

System," Dawson retorted. "Don't tell me you don't have access to the information I want."

"Sorry, but that's what I'm telling you. You don't have to like it, but that doesn't change the facts."

Dawson stared at him with a disappointed look and shook his head. "Fine. The hard way it is then." He stepped forward and whipped the pistol against the side of Hoffman's head. Steel cracked against skull and it all went dark.

———

When Hoffman awoke, he didn't know how long he had been unconscious, but it didn't seem like too much time had passed. The sun was coming in through the east window, so it was still morning. He was naked, gagged, and tied to a chair in the kitchen. His vision blurred in and out of focus from the blow to his head as well as the remnants of last night's drunken debauchery, but he could still see Dawson standing over him.

"Good, you're awake," the mobster said. "Let's get down to business. Remember, you made me do this." He plucked a serrated steak knife from a wooden rack on the counter and used it to sever Hoffman's left pinky finger. It took some serious sawing action to force the blade through the bone, but the knuckle joint split open eventually. The pain was excruciating, unlike anything he could have ever imagined. The gag muffled his screams but did nothing to stop the tears streaming from his eyes.

It was over in less than a minute but felt like an

eternity. His blood dripped onto the kitchen tiles as Dawson tossed his chopped-off finger onto the counter. It bounced to a stop next to the coffee maker. Hoffman felt like he was going to puke. His vision narrowed and blurred into a long, dark tunnel. He felt unconsciousness rushing up from the abyss to claim him again, but before he could succumb to the merciful blackness, a hard slap across the face jolted him back to the here and now.

"Stay with us, Leonard," Dawson said. "You've got nine more fingers to go. Unless, of course, you just want to cooperate and cough up the information." The mobster shrugged. "The choice is yours."

Stay strong, Leonard. Stay strong. Don't give this bastard anything.

Hoffman knew he wasn't the most alpha of males or the kind of rugged, steadfast agent that would never break no matter what torture they inflicted on him. But neither was he some kind of cowardly weakling that would just roll over and piss himself at the first hint of pain. Did it hurt? Yeah, it fucking hurt. It hurt like a real bitch. But it would take more than the loss of a pinkie to get him to talk.

He stared Dawson straight in the eye and though it was muffled by the gag, he growled, "Fuck you."

Dawson smirked. "Tough guy, huh? Okay, we'll play it your way. Fuck me, you say? You won't be fucking anything for the rest of your miserable life." His gaze dropped to Hoffman's naked crotch. "You've got about three seconds before I cut your dick off."

Oh, God, no! Hoffman squirmed in his chair, thrashing his head frantically from side to side. All thoughts about being a badass fled at the thought of the steak knife hacking through his manhood.

"You're shaking your head no," Dawson said. "But I need you to say yes. Yes, you'll give me the information I want. Is that what you're saying?"

Hoffman collected himself enough to stop shaking his head and start nodding instead. *Yes! Yes, I'll do what you want.*

"Smart choice." Dawson signaled to one of his men. "Henry here will remove your gag. If you scream or spit or pull any dumb shit like that, your pathetic dick will be on the counter next to your pinkie. Got it?"

Hoffman nodded. He was in full compliance mode, his spirit broken. The thought of castration was more than he could take. As soon as the gag came off, he gulped some air into his lungs and blurted, "Promise me that you won't kill me."

Dawson tapped the bloody knife against Hoffman's chin. "Give me the information I asked for without any funny business and I promise I won't kill you."

"I need my laptop. It's on the coffee table in the living room. I can remote access into the system from here."

One of the henchmen—not Henry—fetched the computer. They untied his hands so he could type on the keyboard but left his ankles bound to the chair. No more explicit threats were made, but they didn't need to be. With three gunmen watching him closely with itchy trigger fingers—not to mention Dawson with the goddamned steak knife—Hoffman knew that any attempt to do anything with his freed hands other than work the computer would be met with severe consequences.

He remoted into the BOP's Central Inmate Monitoring System with a PIV card and a series of complex passwords and quickly accessed Dawson's file. His fingers—all remaining nine of them—clacked away at the keys, drilling deep into the digital folder. The minutes passed with the sluggish speed of cold molasses flowing uphill.

"You stall, you die," Dawson warned. "If I suspect for even a single second that you're messing with me, you'll die choking on your own dick."

"I'm not stalling," Hoffman protested. "It just takes time."

"Get it sorted or time is something you'll run out of," Dawson replied.

Another minute crawled by, every second feeling like an eternity to Hoffman. Beads of nervous sweat popped out from the pores on his forehead and his heart jackhammered in his chest. He silently prayed that Dawson was telling the truth about letting him live if he gave them the information they wanted.

Ninety seconds later, he had the name.

"Got it," he said, breathing a sigh of relief. "The US Marshal assigned to your wife is Cade Rogers."

"Ex," Dawson said.

"What?"

"I don't have a wife. I have an ex-wife. One who is soon going to be ex-terminated." He chuckled at his own play on words and then asked, "You got an address for this Rogers?"

Hoffman shook his head. "We wouldn't have that information."

Dawson shrugged and tossed the knife onto the counter. "No worries. We'll get it somewhere else." He put his finger in the air and whirled it around in the universal sign for *move out.* "Break time's over, boys. Time to get back on the road."

As the men started to make their way toward the front door, Hoffman felt his hopes go up a few notches. Maybe he was going to survive this after all. And all he'd had to do was betray his oath. Not that hard, really. When it came right down to brass tacks, he would rather be known as a living traitor than a dead hero. That heroic sacrifice shit was overrated.

Dawson paused at the door and turned to the gunman at the back of the line. "Henry, do the honors."

Hoffman felt panic flutter in his chest as his hopes sank like a torpedoed rowboat.

"Sorry, Lenny," Dawson said. "No hard feelings, but...no witnesses."

"You promised you wouldn't kill me."

"And I keep my promises." Dawson's lips curled into a cruel grin. "That's why Henry will kill you, not me."

Hoffman had time for a single scream before Henry plucked the knife from the counter and plunged it into his throat.

TWELVE

STONE SAT in his Chevy Blazer outside the sheriff's station and steeled himself for all the work that lay ahead. For such a small town, Whisper Falls seemed to pony up its fair share of problems. The death of Preston Daggett was just the latest. For some reason, the other towns in Garrison County didn't seem to attract this much violence.

Maybe that's why you were called here, an inner voice suggested. *God sends the warrior to fight evil wherever it takes root.*

Stone shrugged off the thought. While he was slowly learning to live with his dark compulsion to dispense primal justice as well as all the questionable justifications that accompanied the bloodshed, he still felt discomfited when he unleashed the warrior within.

Hell, maybe that's the way it should be, he told himself. Maybe a man of God should never truly be comfortable with killing, no matter the reason. Maybe all the bullets and blood should chip away at his soul.

Problem was, too much chipping away and his soul would cease to exist.

He climbed out of the truck. It was earlier than he usually showed up for work, the sky caught between black and gray, the darkness reluctant to give way to the rising sun. The autumn air had a crisp bite, and his breath plumed like smoke in the cold. It made him miss Texas.

Inside his office, he poured himself a cup of coffee. He had slept like crap last night and would definitely need the caffeine to muddle through the day. As he sat down in his chair, he considered calling a buddy to come guard Holly and Lizzy until Jack Dawson was back behind bars. Gerry Braxx—or G-Man, as his friends called him—was a short fireplug of a guy whose unassuming demeanor concealed the fact that he was a stone-cold killer when the situation called for it. As a martial arts expert, Braxx preferred to use his hands and feet, but was perfectly willing to go to guns if necessary.

They had been through hell together—the six weeks they had spent in a Syrian prison had been particularly brutal—and Stone knew Braxx would lay down his life for him, no questions asked. That was the kind of bond they shared. In other words, the perfect guy to guard the people Stone cared about most in the world.

He kicked the idea around for a few minutes but then discarded it. Braxx had walked away from the killing fields nearly two years before Stone got out, settling down for a normal life with his wife and two sons. Stone had no wish to drag him back into the game.

Besides, the odds of Dawson being able to unearth his ex-wife's new name and location were extremely low, and if at any point it looked like she was compromised, the US Marshals would roll into town to protect her themselves. Stone also doubted Holly would appreciate having a stranger follow her around, even one he vouched for. But he did make a mental note to check in with Braxx once things had settled down. He hadn't seen his friend since Jasmine's funeral.

A little after 0900 hours, he spotted Catfish out in the hallway with a powdered donut dangling from his mouth, his uniform shirt unbuttoned and hanging open.

"Hey, deputy?"

Catfish did an about-face with military precision, stepped into the office, and removed the donut from his mouth. "You rang, sir?" Powder drifted down onto his white undershirt like coke falling from an addict's nose.

"What's with the open shirt? You planning on auditioning down at the Spicy Taco when Lepper gets it open?"

"Just trying not to get powder all over my uniform, boss."

"You ever thought about trying a plain donut instead?"

Catfish held the donut up like it was some kind of

treasure. "They had these in the mess hall every morning without fail over in the sandbox, sir. After four tours, I kind of got addicted to 'em. The plain ones just don't get it done."

Stone understood. He was a Boston cream fan himself. He switched subjects.

"You're a hunter, right?"

The deputy nodded. "Ever since I was a toddler down in the bayou. Gators, mostly, but I've done killed 'bout anything that walks, crawls, swims, or slithers."

"You poke the animal in the eye with your gun barrel after you shoot it to make sure it's dead?"

"Every time, all the time," Catfish replied. "I don't care if it's a snake, gator, or deer, last thing you want is to have some critter you thought was dead popping back to life when you least expect it. Seen it happen with a gator once. My greenhorn cousin forgot to do the eye-poke and it turned out the gator wasn't quite expired." He shook his head. "My cousin ended up with sixty-five stitches and one less testicle."

"Really?"

"Would I lie, sir?" Catfish had a twinkle in his eye.

"Don't make me answer that." Stone pushed back his chair and stood up.

"Going somewhere?" Catfish asked.

"Scratching an itch," Stone replied as he shrugged on his rancher's coat and settled his Stetson on his head.

"Strip club ain't open yet." Catfish grinned.

"Not that kind of itch."

"So where you going?"

"The taxidermist."

Catfish looked confused but nodded anyway. "Makes perfect sense."

———

Inside The Right Stuff Taxidermy shop, Stone was greeted by the typical knotty-pine-and-antler motif that all rural taxidermy shops seemed to favor. The display in the plate glass window at the front of the store featured a full-sized whitetail buck hopping over a barbed wire fence with a wild turkey strutting off to the right and a pheasant perched on a fallen log to the left. It was impressive work, on par with some of the best taxidermists Stone had seen in Texas, and proved that Tom Benson was no slouch at his trade.

The shop itself was crammed full of mounts, every square inch of wall space occupied by some kind of dead animal. Raccoons, coy-wolves, black bears, foxes, deer heads, northern pike, smallmouth bass, bobcats...hell, there was even a bat hanging upside down from a stick in the back corner. Stone knew that right before Halloween, the bat moved closer to the front door and dangled among fake cobwebs to "scare" the customers. He suspected Benson got more amusement out of it than the customers did.

It was early, so there was no one else in the shop. Benson stood behind the counter as if manning the cash register, a cup of coffee in one hand, a cigarette in the other. He wore a camouflaged smock stained with bits of animal flesh and hair. With his sagging face and bleary eyes, he looked like he had slept even worse than Stone last night.

"What's up, Sheriff?" Benson took a swig of coffee and immediately followed it up with a drag on his Marlboro, the tip flaring red for a moment. He then tapped the ash into an ashtray shaped like a bear's paw that sat next to the register.

"Morning," Stone greeted.

"That it is." Benson took another drag and tapped more ash. Smoke drifted up around the ceiling like fog.

"You got a minute to talk?"

Benson smirked and gestured around the empty store. "As you can see, Sheriff, I'm kind of busy right now."

"I'll try to keep it short."

"What's on your mind?" Benson stubbed out his cigarette, set down his coffee, and pulled his long hair into a ponytail that he tied off with a rubber band. It hung down almost to his waist, like it hadn't been cut since the '80s. It also looked kind of greasy, like it hadn't been washed in several days. He leaned forward and rested his elbows on the counter. Just past the edge of his smock, Stone could see the outline of Benson's ribs moving beneath his shirt. The bags under the man's eyes were deep and dark, like someone had pressed their thumbs hard into his flesh and left bruises.

Stone gave the taxidermist a long, piercing look. "Everything okay with you, Tom?"

"That what you came over here to ask me?"

"No, but I'm asking anyway."

Benson's shoulders drooped and he let out a burdened sigh. "Judy is sick. Like, *really* sick. The cancer…well, it's really taking a toll on her. It's so frustrating not being able to do anything to help her."

"Sorry to hear that."

"To be honest, it's putting all kinds of strain on us. Not just on her, but on our marriage, the business… hell, on our sanity. The bills are piling up deeper than the snow on Mount Everest and I've got no idea how to pay 'em." Benson abruptly held up a hand. "And please don't tell me to pray, preacher. I'm not praying to a God that seems to have forsaken us."

"I'll do the praying, Tom. You just take care of Judy."

Benson nodded. "Fair enough. Now, what's on your mind?"

"The buck that Preston Daggett shot, the one that gored him to death…it was brought here, right?"

"Sure was." Benson's eyes narrowed. "It's got Steve Lepper's tag on it. He said you gave the authorization. That so?"

Stone nodded. "Yeah, I let him claim the buck."

"All right, just making sure. The greedy son of a bitch will probably sell the head to Bass Pro Shops or someplace like that. They pay good money for world-class trophies like that, and Lepper has never been one to turn down a dollar."

"Told me he's having it mounted out of respect for Daggett. Didn't sound like he planned on selling it."

"Yeah, well, I guess we'll just see about that," Benson said. "When it comes to Lepper, greed is king."

Stone ignored the insult—Benson was entitled to

his opinion—and asked the question that had brought him here. "Any chance you still have the eyeballs from that buck?"

"Yeah, I haven't touched the head yet."

"Can I get a look at them?"

Benson looked puzzled but shrugged and said, "Sure, come on back."

In the back of the shop, where all the grisly work was done, Benson took the giant buck's head out of the walk-in cooler and set it down on a stainless-steel table. The taxidermist handled the specimen with more than a touch of respect.

"I haven't caped it out yet," Benson said. "Caping basically means taking the hide off the skull. I usually freeze it for a few days before I do that to make sure all the ticks are dead."

"Ticks a big problem this time of the year?"

"You'd be surprised. They're hardy little bastards."

Looking the buck over again, Stone remained impressed by the hugeness of the rack, the mass and girth and symmetry of the tines all working together to create something magnificent. But the deer's natural beauty was marred by the blood stains streaking the antlers.

Daggett killed the buck and then the buck killed him, Stone thought. *Such is the savage circle of life sometimes. One moment you're the hunter, the next moment, you're the hunted.*

It was a lesson Stone knew well from his years spent in kill-zones all over the world.

He looked over at Benson. The taxidermist's eyes were bright with excitement. He seemed to truly love his work and Stone suspected it was a way for him to put the sadness of his wife's disease out of his mind for at least a few brief, stolen moments.

Benson ran his hand almost lovingly over the tuft of fur between the buck's horns. "I learned how to do taxidermy from my father," he said, his voice low and almost reverent, like a worshipper in church on Sunday morning. "He taught me that if you don't respect the animal, if there's no emotion when you recreate life from death, then the customers will be able to tell. He said the only way to make the animals look real is to *feel* it."

Stone glanced around the workspace. While it wouldn't exactly pass for a surgical room, it was cleaner than he had expected. A long, Formica-topped bench ran along the wall to his right, the tools of the trade—knives, scalpels, clay, paintbrushes, and such— laid out in a fairly orderly fashion. Mounts in various stages of completion were seemingly everywhere, and Styrofoam mannequins were piled in every corner, waiting for a hide to be stretched over them.

Benson continued to massage the buck's skullcap, almost as if lost in a trance.

Stone cleared his throat. "Uh, Tom? The eyes?"

"Oh, yeah, right." Benson let out a little laugh. He picked up a scalpel and got to work, removing the deer's eyes with the sure, fluid strokes of a practiced professional. Severed from their connective tissue, they fell onto the bench like grapes. Benson put down the scalpel and picked them up. Nestled in his palm, he held them out to Stone.

Stone looked down at the scooped-out eyeballs for

a long moment, then lifted his gaze to Benson. "Think you could put them in a plastic bag or something for me? Not sure I want to walk around with raw eyeballs shoved in my pocket."

"Sure thing, Sheriff. You taking them somewhere?"

"Yeah," Stone replied. "The coroner."

THIRTEEN

STONE HAD SEEN HUNDREDS, maybe even thousands, of corpses during his warrior days, most of them torn and twisted and disfigured by some kind of violent death, so the sight of the pale-skinned dead woman on the morgue slab wasn't unduly upsetting. Nor was the gaping hole in the back of her head where the .357 Magnum bullet had exited after she shoved the barrel in her mouth and pulled the trigger. Stone recognized the woman from the suicide scene he'd been summoned to earlier this week, just two days before Preston Daggett got himself gored by a trophy buck.

Her flesh was waxen, white as a maggot's underbelly, and the long, dark lashes contrasted against it starkly, as did the thick layer of black mascara that ringed her eyes like a raccoon.

Andy Cooper, the Garrison County Coroner who had taken the position after the previous one was murdered as part of a child sex-trafficking ring coverup, looked up as Stone walked in and held out the bag containing the buck's eyeballs. "Something I can do for you, Sheriff?" He carefully set down his autopsy tools, the metal utensils making a soft clink against the stainless-steel table.

Stone got right to the point. "Can you tell me if there's gunpowder residue on one of these eyeballs?"

"Of course. Shouldn't be much of an issue."

"Any idea how long it'll take?"

"Should have an answer for you later today, tomorrow at the latest." Cooper always worked fast for Stone, since Stone had paid to modernize the facilities out of his own pocket once he became sheriff. He had figured it was a good use of some of the blood money he had accumulated during his warrior days, and Cooper returned the favor by not making him wait long for test results.

Stone gestured at the corpse. "Still sure it's a suicide?"

Cooper nodded. "No doubt about it. You still sure Preston Daggett was an accident?"

"Looks that way."

"Yet you're still bringing me deer eyeballs in a sandwich bag."

"Just scratching an itch."

"God help us." Cooper made a face. "When you get an itch, I get busy."

Stone gave him a slight smile, conceding that there might be a smidgen of truth in the statement. But before he could say anything, his cell phone buzzed. He fished it from his pocket and checked the caller ID.

It was Holly. "Excuse me, Andy," he said. "I've gotta take this."

"Sure, no problem."

Stone answered. "Hey, Holly, what's up?" He could hear the sounds of the diner where she worked in the background.

"Sorry to bother you, but..."

"Whatever it is, it's no bother, I promise."

"Any chance you have some time to talk to Lizzy?"

"I'll make time. What's going on?"

Holly sighed. "She claimed she was sick this morning, but it was pretty obvious that it was just an excuse to skip school. I can tell something is wrong but she won't talk to me." A long pause, then: "Luke, it feels like I'm losing her."

"You're not losing her," Stone replied. "She's a teenager. They go through phases. I'll head out there shortly and have a chat with her. I'm sure she's fine. And if she's not, well, maybe I can help her deal with that, too."

"I won't lie, Luke, I'm really worried about her."

"I know you are. I'll check on her."

"Thank you."

"Don't mention it. I'll call you later."

Stone hung up and looked at Cooper. "I've gotta run. Can you email me the results once you know something?"

"Sure thing, Sheriff."

Stone stopped by the sheriff's station on the way out of town and checked on the deputies. Sanchez was covering the desk while Catfish was out on patrol, and Valentine wouldn't be on duty until later. Sanchez informed him it had been a quiet day so far and she hoped it stayed that way. She also told him that Catfish was hoping for the exact opposite because he was bored.

"That guy is a total adrenaline junkie," she said. "Isn't happy unless there's some action."

"Takes all kinds to make the world go round," Stone replied. "I'll be off the clock on a secret mission if anyone's looking for me."

"Top secret shenanigans, huh?" Sanchez laughed. "What are you, some kind of special agent or something?" Her tone was light but the question was partly serious.

The mysteriousness of his past was something of a running joke, not just here at the station but all over town. Everybody had their theories about what he had done before he rode into town, and Stone left them to their speculation without confirmation or denial. Maybe someday he would be comfortable enough to loosen his lips and let people know about his warrior days as a black ops trigger-puller, but not today.

Instead, he just smiled at Sanchez and said, "Something like that."

FOURTEEN

LIZZY CURLED up in bed with the blankets tucked around her like a little kid afraid of monsters. She knew her mother hadn't believed her poorly delivered lie about being sick, but she really didn't care. As long as she didn't have to go to school and face the Macero twins, her mom could be as annoyed as she wanted to be. Conflict avoidance wasn't usually her style—she was generally a fairly self-confident kid who didn't dodge the hard stuff that life threw her way—but in this situation, she just wasn't sure what else to do.

Those bitches were brutal.

Maybe it was time for them to leave Whisper Falls. It wasn't the first time she had thought about it. They were supposed to be safe here, but so far, that had not been the case. They had been targeted for murder by child-trafficking survivalists, her best friend had been burned alive, and she had been kidnapped by a psychopathic narco-queen. The teenage years were supposed to be hard but things were getting ridiculous. All it would take is one call from her mother to the marshals and they would be whisked out of town before dawn, never to be seen around Whisper Falls again.

Right now, that sounded like heaven.

She was wiping away tears when she heard the front door open downstairs. For a moment she panicked, but then she heard a familiar voice call out her name.

"Lizzy, it's Luke. You home?"

She really wasn't in the mood for company and thought about not answering, but she knew Stone wouldn't leave without searching the entire house. Better to just get this over with.

"In my bedroom," she replied, raising her voice to make sure he heard her.

She heard his footsteps coming up the stairs and down the hall. "You decent?" he asked.

"What if I'm not?"

"Then I'll wait out here until you are."

Lizzy rolled her eyes, shook her head, and said, "I'm good. You can come in."

He nudged open the door with his foot. "Thought maybe we could talk."

"Whatever."

"You hungry? We could go get something to eat, chat over some food."

"I don't feel like going anywhere." She threw off the blanket. "I'll make us sandwiches." She rolled off the bed, shoved her feet into some slippers, and headed for the door, brushing past him. "Follow me."

He trailed her down into the kitchen, where she

fished a package of deli meat from one of the drawers in the fridge and started slapping honey-glazed ham slices onto some wheat bread. "Mustard or mayo?" she asked.

"I'm good. Just make yourself one."

"I'll bet Jesus wouldn't make me eat alone."

"Playing the Jesus card, huh? Cheap shot." Stone smiled at her. "Okay, make mine with mustard. Putting mayonnaise on ham is some kind of sin."

"Duly noted. You're repulsed by mayo."

She doused his sandwich with enough mustard to turn a whole rainbow yellow, dropped it onto a plate, and shoved it in front of him. "Bon appétit."

She made herself a sandwich—using the mayonnaise out of some kind of immature spite—and took small bites with zero enthusiasm. The food just felt like a dry, tasteless lump in her mouth. The silence created a gulf between them, and while part of her didn't give a damn, another part wondered why the gulf was there. Luke was a great listener, and usually, she could talk to him without any problem. And *about* any problem. But right now, she didn't feel like talking to anybody, and that included him.

The silence stretched on, and it was so uncomfortable. At least, it was for her. She couldn't really tell how Stone felt. He had a great poker face when he didn't want you to know what he was thinking. He just ate his sandwich and didn't say anything. Hell, he barely even looked at her, as if that ham sandwich was the only thing in the world worth paying attention to right now.

Finally, she couldn't stand the strained quiet any longer. "I know why you're here," she said.

"Figured you did."

"I'm not stupid, you know."

"Never said you were."

"My mom sent you to talk to me, right?"

Stone nodded. "She's worried about you. Moms get like that when their daughters stop talking to them all of a sudden."

Lizzy shoved away her half-eaten sandwich and crossed her arms. "Yeah, okay. Whatever."

"Why don't you just tell me what's bothering you and save us both some time?"

She couldn't help but smile a little at his bluntness. "Typical Luke," she said. "Cut the bullshit and get right down to the meat and bone of the matter."

"Bullshit rarely does anyone much good," Stone replied.

"I've just been having some trouble at school. Nothing I can't handle, nothing to worry about. Satisfied?"

"That why you faked being sick today?"

"I think you have to read me my rights before you interrogate me. Isn't that how it works?"

"Stop being a drama queen," Stone said. "Doesn't suit you. I think by now I've proven I only want to help you."

"Like I said, it's nothing," Lizzy replied. "Just some girls at school being total bitches. You know, giving me some hassle. Nothing for you or my mother to worry about."

"Are they hurting you?"

She hesitated, a denial ripe and ready to go resting on the tip of her tongue. But then she changed her mind, shrugged, and said, "A little."

"Show me."

Reluctantly, she raised her sweatshirt enough to expose the purple-yellow bruising tattooed across her battered ribs and stomach. She saw a flicker of anger behind Stone's honey-colored eyes and his lips tightened into a thin line.

"That's more than a little," Stone said.

She lowered her shirt. "I've got it under control."

"That's a bunch of crap and you know it. If you had it under control, you wouldn't look like a herd of cows stampeded over you."

Lizzy threw up her arms in frustration. "What the hell do you want me to do, huh? Tell me, Luke! You want me to fight? That's what you would do, right?" She felt the tears springing into her eyes and despised her weakness. *C'mon, girl, pull yourself together.* This was not who she was, but it was what the Macero twins had reduced her to.

"The only way to deal with bullies is to stand up to them," Stone said. "So yeah, I want you to fight, if that's what it's going to take."

"If I stand up to them, they might just hurt me even worse."

"Even if you lose the fight and they put another beat down on you, they'll at least know you're not gonna take their shit lying down, that you're not someone to mess with. Trust me, bullies prefer victims that don't fight back."

"I guess you're not one of those *turn-the-other-cheek* preachers," Lizzy said with a halfhearted laugh.

Something strange—and dangerous—passed like a shadow behind Stone's eyes. There one heartbeat, gone the next. "The Bible says there's a time and place for everything, and I reckon that means fighting as well," he said. "Besides, the same Jesus that said to turn the other cheek also made a scourge and went all whip-happy in the temple. Kind of hard to argue that God's not okay with violence sometimes." He grinned at her. "Besides, turn the other cheek just means that after they hit you twice, all bets are off and it's game time."

"You've got a weird way of interpreting the Bible," she said.

"So I've been told."

"They've got me outnumbered," Lizzy complained. "It's two against one. What can I do against two psychotic bitches?"

"I can give you some pointers, show you some fighting tricks."

She perked up. "Really? That'd be cool."

"But first, tell me who these girls are."

"Why? So you can go to their house, have a confrontation, and make things even worse?" She shook her head. "No way, not happening."

"I have other ways of finding out, you know."

Lizzy knew the battle was already lost. When Stone wanted to know something, he would dig relentlessly until he figured it out, using any methods he deemed necessary. Better just to tell him what he wanted to know right now and be done with it. "The Macero twins," she said reluctantly.

Stone clearly recognized the name. "Their dad just got out of prison."

"Yeah, I'm aware," she replied. "They talk about it all the time. They almost seem proud of the fact that their father is an ex-con."

"Maybe they think it gives them some kind of street cred."

"Yeah, well, I don't care about their stupid street cred. I just want them both in a coffin."

"Well, I'm not going to teach you how to kill them," Stone replied. "But let's go out back and I'll show you some moves like a knee-smash, shin-rake, and groin strike."

Lizzy grinned at him. "Pretty sure you're not supposed to offer a groin strike to a girl my age."

"You're wicked, you know that? Put some shoes on and meet me outside."

She ran back upstairs, swapped the sweatshirt she was currently wearing for an older, rattier one, and threw on some old hiking boots before joining Stone in the backyard. The air was brisk and smelled of pine needles from the trees that grew along the edge of the property.

"The first piece of advice I'm going to give you," Stone said, "is to avoid the fight if at all possible. Don't engage with them unless they engage with you. If there's a way to avoid a confrontation, take it."

"So I should just run away?"

"More like just walk away. I'm not telling you to act like a coward, but I'm not telling you to draw first blood either. If they'll give you a chance to walk away, take it."

"Live to fight another day."

"Something like that," Stone said. "Don't escalate the situation yourself. Force them to be the aggressors. But if they won't let you walk away, then don't back down. Just like animals, human predators target those they consider weak and vulnerable."

"Well, isn't that just great." Lizzy let her shoulders slump. "Now I'm weak and vulnerable."

"No, you're not," Stone said firmly. "But the Macero twins *think* you are, which is why they keep coming for you. You need to prove them wrong, show them that you're not an easy mark. They're not looking for a fight, they're looking for a target."

Lizzy crossed her arms. "You make it sound so simple, but it's not."

"It's simple and hard at the same time," Stone replied. "But that's the way life works."

"Yeah, well, life sucks sometimes."

"You're preaching to the choir, kid."

Her face softened as she looked at him. "I know you've been through some shit, Luke."

"Everybody goes through some shit, Liz."

"You want to show me how to get through mine without ending up in the hospital? Telling me not to back down to those bitches only works if I know how to defend myself."

Stone spent the next forty-five minutes demonstrating various hand-to-hand fighting techniques. He ran Lizzy through some drills, correcting her form where necessary and helping her learn some basic combat skills. She studied his movements intensely, soaking it all in so that she could practice again later, alone in her room.

"Man, I feel like a ninja or something," she said, executing a heel-palm strike that was a long way from flawless but a whole lot better than it had been thirty minutes ago. "Now how about you teach me that groin strike thing you were talking about?"

"Maybe you should practice your shin-rakes some more. They need some work," Stone said. "Besides, do you really need a lesson in how to kick somebody in the crotch?"

Lizzy grinned. "I guess I can figure that one out on my own."

"Good." Stone clamped down his Stetson and headed for the truck. "Because I've got something I need to do."

FIFTEEN

STONE KNEW BETTER than to make hasty judgments about people, but he thought Vance Macero might be an exception to that particular rule. Sometimes people are exactly what you think they are. He'd done hard time in prison, he was a mean drunk who was perfectly willing to throw fists, and he had raised bully daughters. Slap it all together and it didn't add up to the man being a model citizen.

Still, Stone had no intention of immediately resorting to violence. He would start by having a friendly chat with the man, let him know where things stood. But he strongly suspected things would get unfriendly real fast. Men—even bad men—didn't like it when you talked shit about their daughters.

The Macero residence was a single-wide trailer with peeling paint and dark mold stains in the corners to accompany the rust, squatting in the middle of a stand of half-dead pine trees. Debris and junk filled the unkempt yard, the lawn more weeds than grass, and all of it at least knee-high. One more good rain and they would need a machete to tame the jungle-like underbrush, not a mower.

As Stone approached the trailer, he saw the front door was partially open despite the cool weather, pungent marijuana smoke drifting out through the gap. He spotted Vance sitting around a card table with two teenage girls—his daughters, presumably—playing cards. A bottle of beer perched on the table next to his elbow. There were no visible signs of the beat down Stone had put on him a couple nights ago at the Nailed Coffin, save maybe for the smoldering hate in his eyes.

"Cops ain't welcome 'round these parts," Vance growled as Stone stepped up onto the small porch made out of rotting 2x4s. "And I know for a damn fact that I don't have to talk to no law dog if I don't want to."

"Always good to meet a man who knows his rights," Stone said dryly.

"Am I under arrest or something?"

"Not yet, but the day is young and the possibilities are endless."

"What do you want?"

"Don't talk to the pig," one of the girls said.

"Yeah, tell him to pound salt," the other girl chimed in.

"Shut up, both of you," Vance snapped. He fixed his hard, bloodshot eyes on Stone. "Well?"

"Just want to have a chat with you, that's all," Stone said. "Won't take long."

Vance studied him for a moment and then asked, "You got a warrant?"

"Don't need a warrant for a chat."

"If you ain't got no warrant, then you can drag your sorry ass outta here and hit the road."

"Maybe you could just step outside so we can get this over with."

"What in the ever-lovin' fuck do you and me got to talk about?" Vance demanded.

"Be better if we had that conversation outside." Stone's eyes flicked to the twin girls and then settled back on Vance. "Alone."

Vance heaved an exasperated sigh and threw down his cards in disgust. Petra and Nova started to protest but a harsh glare quieted them. They might be bullies at school, but Vance clearly ruled the roost here at home. He pushed back from the table, drained the beer, slammed down the bottle, and then walked to the door. "Sure, fine, Sheriff. Whatever it takes to get you the hell outta my hair and the fuck off my property."

They stepped outside and drew up next to a square-body Ford pickup resting on cracked cinder blocks, the truck held together by not much more than rust and Bondo. Vance's plaid shirt looked like it had lost a war with an army of moths, drooping off his thin but hard-muscled frame. Stone visually scanned the ex-con, looking for any sign of weapons.

Vance caught the look. "You can search me if it'll make you feel better," he said with a sneer. "I'm not carrying shit. No drugs, no guns, not even a frigging pocket knife. I know the conditions of my parole and I ain't going back to the slammer."

"No drugs, huh?" The corner of Stone's mouth tugged up in a wry, mirthless smile. "Guess that's cigarette smoke I smell coming out of your trailer."

"Burned spaghetti sauce," Vance deadpanned with a perfect poker face. "Petra overcooked the Ragu."

"Relax," Stone said. "I'm not here to bust you over some weed."

"Then what the hell *are* you here for?"

"Need to talk to you about your girls."

Vance cocked an eyebrow. "For real?"

"They're being bullies at school, hurting other students."

"Yeah, and what of it? The world ain't all sunshine and roses, lawman, and kids will be kids."

"That's no excuse for physical assault."

Vance snorted in disgust. "I can't believe you're hassling me about my girls getting into a few scuffles at school. Don't you have nothin' better to do? Parking tickets to write or something?"

"I'll decide what to do with my time, not you."

Vance turned his head, hawked up the phlegm in his throat, and spat the globule under the decrepit truck before looking back at Stone. "This alleged victim, or victims, or whoever the hell is yappin' in your ear...did they file formal charges against my daughters?"

"Not yet, and I'm hoping it doesn't come to that."

"You know what, lawman? You're full of shit. Either tell me who the accuser is or fuck off."

"Doesn't matter." Stone's eyes shifted to Petra and

Nova huddled in the doorway, eavesdropping on the conversation. "Your girls know who they've been pounding on, and it needs to stop."

"This stupid crap is starting to feel like police harassment," Vance said. "I think we're done here. Time for you to get back in your truck and mosey on down the highway."

Petra piped up. "It's that Lizzy Bennett spreading these lies about us, Daddy."

Vance glanced at his daughter and then looked back at Stone. "The Bennett bitch? Seriously? That little purple-haired emo freak?"

"I'm not here to discuss the victim," Stone replied. "I'm here to make sure she's not a victim anymore."

"Get the hell off my property, Sheriff."

"Not until we come to an understanding about your daughters' behavior."

"You banging this Lizzy tramp, is that it?" Vance grinned lasciviously. "She like the handcuffs, does she?"

Stone decided he'd played nice long enough. "You should probably shut your mouth."

"Or what?" Vance took a step forward with his fists clenched.

"Or I'll kick your teeth down your throat, haul your ass back to jail, and toss your abusive little daughters into the foster care system."

Vance's eyes narrowed to hot, angry, glittering slits. "Nobody talks to me like that, motherfucker." He swung wildly and without warning, his hard-knuckled right fist coming up and around.

It was a fast strike, the speed no doubt acquired

from dozens of prison yard brawls, and had it connected, it would have hurt like hell. But Stone had been anticipating the punch and easily dodged to the side, letting the blow slice past his head. He saw the rage, the burning fury, heating up Vance's face and knew the ex-con had lost all self-control. The man was in beast mode, relying on his primitive, violent instincts.

Vance's next swing was a little closer but still easily avoided. Stone lashed out with his boot and executed a hard leg sweep that dumped Vance on his bony ass. He hit the ground with a thump and a curse. Stone hoped the man would have the good sense to stay down.

No such luck.

As Vance scrabbled to his feet, the twins rushed out onto the porch and clutched the railing. "Daddy!" they both cried out in unison.

"Stay out of this, girls," Vance snapped, not even looking their way, his eyes fixed on Stone like a heat-seeking missile locked on target. He lunged forward, throwing a roundhouse punch.

Stone stepped back, felt the blow brush past the tip of his nose. That punch had been even faster than the first two. Looked like Vance was just getting warmed up, finding his speed and rhythm.

Vance hauled his arm back for another punch, but Stone struck first, stepping in and firing a stiff-fingered jab into the ex-con's exposed throat. Not hard enough to kill but plenty hard enough to get the man's attention.

Vance staggered backward, clutching his bruised Adam's apple and sputtering out a string of gagging noises punctuated by four-letter obscenities. He bounced off the rear quarter panel of the cinder-blocked Ford, tripped over an old muffler in the weeds, and went down on his ass for the second time.

"Daddy!" the twins cried out again. But they stayed put on the porch.

"Vance," Stone said, "this isn't a cop-to-con thing, this is a man-to-man thing. So from one man to another, don't pick a fight you can't win. And if your girls don't back off from Lizzy Bennett, I'll consider that you picking a fight." He injected steel into his voice with his next words. "And Vance, that's a fight you won't win."

Vance struggled to reclaim his breathing, the sound like a file rasping against bone. He didn't respond to Stone's threat, too busy massaging his hurting throat.

"You'll be fine in another minute or two," Stone said. "But I meant what I said, Vance. Don't make me come back here. Since you can't talk right now, just nod if you understand me."

The ex-con's head jerked up and down as he coughed in pain, his eyes watering.

"Fuck you, pig!" Petra screamed as her sister shot him the middle finger. "You tell that bitch Lizzy that she'll be sucking cocks in hell before I'm done with her!"

"Nice kids you got there," Stone said to Vance.

He walked back to his truck, started the engine, and gunned the gas. Rooster tails ripped out from under the Blazer's tires and sprayed Vance with dust and gravel as he drove away with the twins' curses and threats chasing him down the road.

SIXTEEN

JACK DAWSON STOOD outside US Marshal Cade Roger's house, spackled with blood and dirt, knowing the sparse moonlight wasn't enough to reveal him and his trio of trigger-pullers hiding in the dark pool of shadows beneath the massive shade tree. His eye—or rather, the mangled socket that had once held his eye—hurt like he was being skull-fucked with a branding iron. He made a mental note to pop some more painkillers when he was done with the marshal. Not enough to dull his senses, just enough to take the edge off.

Through the window that provided a view into the kitchen, they watched the woman inside, washing dishes, her arms in soapy water up to her elbows. He heard the three men behind him making lewd remarks that made them sound more like horny teenagers than the professionals they were.

She was a looker, all right, no doubt about that. The nanny, presumably. Young, blonde, with ample breasts and tight clothes that would be an absolute joy to tear off, especially after all those years in the slammer with no conjugal activity. He probably wouldn't last ten seconds with her, but that didn't matter. It would be about his pleasure, not hers. He felt himself becoming aroused and forced himself to focus on the issue at hand.

Information first, then playtime.

The wife and young boy were upstairs, tucked away in their beds, the windows dark. The lights had been switched off at least fifteen minutes ago.

Dawson watched as the nanny flicked the dishwater off her hands and then dried them on a towel draped over her shoulder. Her presence was an obstacle he had not planned for but not one that caused him much concern. She was a speed bump, nothing more—and a pleasurable one at that—and he would roll right over her when the time came. Or rather, *onto* her.

God, he had been behind bars too long.

No sign of the marshal yet. The man was running late. But they would make themselves at home until he showed up. He and his soldiers could certainly handle a nanny, wife, and little kid.

Dawson glanced up at the dark sky again. Crickets called in the shadows as clouds shrouded the moon.

Yeah, it was a good night for a killing.

———

Cade drove home and tried not to think about the new nanny, hired after the previous one died three weeks ago. Her name was Gina and for a man like Rogers, fast approaching fifty, she was an unwelcome temptation to have around the house. Their last nanny had been old enough to babysit Jesus, and while she had done a great job helping them with the cooking and cleaning and raising their son Bryson, she hadn't exactly been much in the eye-candy department. Rogers still could not believe his wife had replaced her with a tight young thing like Gina. Seriously, what was she thinking? Maybe she was testing him.

As he pulled into his driveway, Rogers saw that every light in the house was on again and mouthed a curse. Gina might be smoking hot and ready-to-trot, but she was dumber than a lobotomized cat. He had warned her at least half a dozen times about minimizing the number of lights on at night to cut down the electric bill. She would just smile as he scolded her, bite her lower lip with all the subtlety of a porn star, and promise to make it up to him as she reached for his zipper.

Gonna have to fire her, Rogers thought. *She doesn't listen worth a damn and I do not want to cheat on my wife.*

He needed a cold beer. Hell, he'd settle for a warm beer at this point. It had been a long day.

The gravel in his driveway crackled under his car tires as he pulled up to the garage. Someday he would be able to afford blacktop but probably not until they were done spending a small fortune on nannies because his wife's medical condition prevented her from being able to properly care for Bryson. Parkinson's disease was such a bitch, and he had no idea why in hell God would inflict it upon anybody, let alone a sweet woman like Katherine. If that was the reward for being a devout Catholic, Rogers figured he would just stick with being an atheist. Not that he would tell Kathy that, she still believed he was agnostic.

He cut the motor, switched off the headlights, and just sat there for a few moments, trying to find some semblance of peace in the quiet of the night. He had been on high alert since Jack 'Lucky Draw' Dawson had managed a ballsy, bloody escape from federal prison.

He still found it hard to believe the guy hadn't been caught yet. Not that he was too worried, as it would be next to impossible for the mobster to track down his ex-wife and daughter without knowing their new identities and location. He knew Dawson wanted revenge, but Rogers remained confident that the people he was responsible for protecting were safe. Maybe the WITSEC program's overall track record wasn't perfect, but his personal record was. He had never lost a charge, and he didn't intend to start now. There was a reason he received glowing performance evaluations from his superiors. They trusted him to do his job and to do it well.

He took a deep breath and opened the car door. As he swung his legs out, he felt his duty-carry Glock dig into his side, riding in a leather paddle holster concealed by his jacket. He had a snub-nosed .38 pistol in an ankle rig for backup. He'd only drawn the Glock once in the line of duty. The snubby had never seen action. And a lack of action was fine with him, especially this close to retirement. No point in giving the government twenty-five good years of your life only to catch a bullet in the brisket when you had one foot out the door.

One thing was for sure, when he retired, he was getting rid of the nanny. He didn't need the temptation or the expense. He would take care of Katherine and Bryson himself.

He stepped around to the side door of the house, fumbling for the key that would let him in. As soon as the lock clicked open, he heard a thump coming from the kitchen, like something hard hitting the floor. He shook his head. Probably Gina dropping a can of Diet Coke. The girl was so klutzy that Rogers got nervous letting her chop vegetables, afraid that one day the fingerling potatoes would end up with an actual finger in them.

Is this some kind of homemade vinaigrette on the salad, Gina?

Why, no, Mr. Rogers. That's just the blood from my severed pinkie.

He shook his head again and stepped into the kitchen, eyes down as he dropped his keys back into his pocket, saying, "You all right, Gina?"

The first thing he saw was the puddle on the floor. Dark and still oozing. Not brown like the spilled cola he had expected, but much more reddish in color.

As he started to raise his eyes, the stench hit his nostrils.

It smelled like a slaughterhouse in here.

Then he saw the four men.

The nearest one leaned his hip against the counter by the sink, one eye covered by a black patch, the other eye unnaturally bright with an evil glow, his arms covered in blood. Rogers didn't need a wanted poster to know who the man was. He would recognize Jack Dawson anywhere.

Gina lay sprawled across the dining room table, naked and gutted, body motionless with the stillness that only death can bring. Her pale skin was splashed with blood, sticky but not yet dried, evidence that her killing had taken place very recently. Her hands were curled into stiff claws from the agony of what they had done to her. Her clothes were scattered across the kitchen, blouse hanging from a corner of the refrigerator, denim shorts wadded up next to the toaster.

The cabinets hung open, some of the doors hanging by a single hinge, torn boxes and broken jars strewn everywhere. It looked like a tornado had ripped through the room.

"Sorry about the mess," Dawson said. "You're late, and we got hungry while we waited for you." He glanced at Gina's ravaged corpse and then back at Rogers. "Hungry and bored, if you know what I mean."

Rogers stared at the most wanted man in America right now and saw nothing but a single shark eye staring back at him. Cold, calculating, soulless, powerful…and utterly dangerous. Dawson had executed dozens, maybe even hundreds, during his Vegas kingpin days. He had orchestrated a bloodbath in order to break out of prison. He had violated and butchered an innocent woman for no other reason than it amused him.

The man was a fucking monster.

"Where are my wife and son?" Rogers asked, doing his best to keep the quiver out of his voice and not entirely sure he succeeded.

"Upstairs and tied to their beds, perfectly safe for now, Mr. Rogers." Dawson grinned. "Mr. Rogers...talk about an unfortunate name. Ain't it just a beautiful fucking day in the neighborhood?"

Rogers briefly considered going for his gun but discarded the thought a second later. He might get one, maybe two of them, but no way in hell would he be able to drop all four before return fire cut him down. As if sensing what he was thinking, one of Dawson's men stepped forward and patted him down, removing both the Glock and the snubby. Rogers didn't fight them. There was no point. Sometimes a man needed to know when he was bested and just let the hand play out and hope for his luck to change.

"What do you want?" he asked.

"Nothing more than your cooperation," Dawson replied. "All you have to do is answer my questions and no harm will come to you, your wife, or your son."

Just hearing the words *wife*, *son*, and *harm* in the same sentence made Rogers' knees want to buckle. He gritted his teeth and forced himself to stand up straight. "What questions?"

Dawson pushed away from the counter he'd been leaning against and strolled over to stand in front of the marshal. "I'm pretty sure you already know the answer to that. You know who I am, so you know the information I'm looking for." He gestured at Gina's gutted corpse. "Give it to me or your precious little wife will look like that."

"If that happens, so help me God, I'll—"

Dawson slapped him hard across the face. "Who the fuck do you think you're talking to, making threats? Huh? You think you're in charge here or something?"

"Listen…"

"No, you listen, Marshal. All I want from you are the new names you gave my ex-wife and daughter and their current location."

Rogers didn't immediately respond, his mind furiously churning, spinning, trying to find some way out of this mess.

Turned out, Dawson's patience was thinner than wet toilet paper. "Go upstairs, cut the boy's head off, and bring it to me like John the fucking Baptist's head on a silver platter," he said to one of his men. "No clean kill, either. Saw it off nice and slow. Make the kid suffer."

"*NO!*" Rogers screamed.

"Give me a reason not to," Dawson replied. "You've got about two seconds."

"I'll do it." Rogers' shoulders slumped. He knew he was giving Holly and Lizzy Bennett a death sentence. "I'll tell you what you want to know."

"Do you need to go fetch your computer?"

"No." Rogers tapped his temple. "I've got it right here. You promise to let my wife and son live?"

"I think I already made that clear."

Rogers didn't know if he could believe the man or not,

but he was out of options. He either gave Dawson what he wanted or his family died, and he wasn't willing to let that happen. "Your wife's name is now Holly Bennett. Your daughter is Eliza. They live just outside Whisper Falls, New York, up in the Adirondack Mountains."

"Holly? Are you kidding me? That's a stupid name. No way she picked that herself. And Eliza? Let me guess, everybody calls her Liz or Lizzy."

Rogers shrugged and nodded. "Yeah, that's usually what happens with that name."

"She got that dumbass name from you." Without warning, Dawson slugged him in the jaw. It felt like getting hit with a sledgehammer. There was a whole lot of pent-up anger behind that blow.

Rogers staggered to the side, catching himself on the counter, but a follow-up punch pummeled him in the stomach, doubling him over. Dawson's knee powered up and connected with Rogers' chin and he found himself flat on the kitchen floor as if trying to make a snow angel in Gina's coagulating blood.

Dawson loomed over him, and now there was a suppressed Beretta pistol in his hand, aimed right at Rogers' face. "You feds never should have fucked with me," he growled. "What happens next is that my men all take a turn with your wife, and then we kill her and the kid. But don't worry, you won't be around to see it."

"You said you'd let them live!" Rogers shouted.

"I did. I let them live until you gave me what I needed. I never promised to let them live forever." Without taking his eyes off Rogers, Dawson said, "Go get 'em and bring 'em down here, boys. The night's about to get wild."

No, no, no, this can't be happening, Rogers thought, panic and horror seizing his heart. *God, no, please don't let this happen.*

He heard the eager thud of boots on stairs, followed by the terrified cries of his wife and the hysterical sobbing of his little boy.

They were the last sounds he ever heard.

When he opened his mouth to scream, Dawson put a bullet down his throat.

SEVENTEEN

STONE SAT at the table in the restaurant of the newly renovated hotel in town and sipped his usual drink as he waited for Holly to show up for their "date" ... or whatever you called it when two members of the opposite sex who were semi-voluntarily trapped in the limbo between friendship and something more got together for dinner. As usual, he was the first to arrive, having been raised by his father that if you're not ten minutes early, then you're late.

Next to him, a floor-to-ceiling window provided a view out onto the sidewalk. Rivulets streamed down the glass like a waterfall, another torrential rainstorm blanketing the area. Not quite as bad as the one from the other night, but close. He hoped Holly remembered a jacket and umbrella this time.

While he waited for her to show up, he looked over the menu. He had just scanned the appetizers, wondering if he should order some maple-roasted brussels sprouts so they would be here when Holly arrived, when his phone vibrated. A glance at the screen showed that it was the coroner calling.

Keeping his voice low out of deference to the other diners in the restaurant, Stone answered. "Hey, Andy. What's up?"

"I have that information you requested," Cooper replied. "Figured you would want me to give you the report ASAP."

"You figured right. Fire away."

"There were traces of gunpowder residue on the buck's eyeball."

"So Daggett *did* check to make sure the buck was dead." Stone paused. "How the hell did he get gored to death then?"

"He didn't," Cooper said. "He was *stabbed* to death."

"I'm listening."

"The autopsy shows that the wound to Mr. Daggett's heart was too clean to have been done by an antler."

"What did it then?"

"Most likely a knife, straight edge, no serrations."

"Like a hunting knife," Stone said.

"Precisely. It appears someone stabbed Daggett in the heart and then forced the antler into the wound to try to cover it up." Cooper sighed. "This wasn't an accidental death, Sheriff…this was a homicide."

"I knew something was off about this case," Stone muttered.

"You've got good instincts."

"What I've got is a murder to solve."

"Sorry to be the bearer of bad news," Cooper said.

"It's not bad news," Stone replied. "It's just the cold, hard truth. And I'll take the truth over a pack of lies any day of the week and twice on Sundays."

"I hear that."

"Thanks, Andy. I'll be in touch."

As Stone hung up the phone, he saw Holly walking into the restaurant through the arched entrance, wearing a blue rain slicker and carrying a closed umbrella that dripped water on the hardwood floor. She gave him a little wave as she made her way over.

"Sorry I'm late," she said as she sat down. She immediately sensed his somber mood. They might not be romantically involved but they spent enough time together to be in tune with each other's emotions. "What's wrong?" she asked.

Stone settled his honey-colored eyes on her and felt something stir inside him. Not for the first time, he cursed whatever unspoken things lurked in their hearts that kept them from moving forward with their relationship. Sometimes—like right now—he felt he was screwing up a damn good thing by not sweeping Holly into his arms. Other times—most of the time—he felt like their friendship was enough.

He shook off the thoughts and answered her question. "I just found out that Preston Daggett's death wasn't an accident. He was murdered."

Her eyes pierced him and he could see in her gaze the same regret and acceptance that he had just been thinking about. She looked like she was about to say something but then seemed to change her mind and settle for something less emotionally risky. "That's horrible," she said. "Are you positive?"

"Coroner confirmed it right before you got here," Stone said. "I need to go break the news to his wife. Do you mind if I take a raincheck on dinner?"

"Of course. Not a problem."

"I feel lousy about it."

"No reason to feel bad. You're just doing your job."

Stone almost said, *You're way more important than my job*, but decided it could be taken wrong, too forward, and make her uncomfortable. Which was the last thing he wanted to do. So instead, he said, "I really am sorry. I'll make it up to you soon."

She smiled, both wistful and understanding. "You damn well better, cowboy."

———

The Daggett residence sat right on the border between Garrison and Essex counties, tucked up on a granite ridge with a private drive that threaded between two gargantuan borders. It was a steep hill, one that Stone reckoned had to be an absolute pain in the ass to plow after a winter snowstorm.

It was quiet up here, and if not for the darkness and the downpour, the view would be spectacular, with Whiteface Mountain looming far in the distance. Stone lived on a remote patch of property himself and understood the appeal of not having neighbors and the privacy of wild land to roam. The Daggett place was so far off the main roads that traffic was negligible, bordering on nonexistent. You were more apt to see a moose wander by than another vehicle.

Which made it surprising when Stone approached the driveway and saw a dark SUV pull out and make a left-hand turn that took it past Stone's Blazer.

Well, that's strange, he thought. But then, it could just be a friend stopping by to drop off a casserole and offer condolences to the grieving widow. Wasn't like much time had passed since Preston's death. Certainly not enough time for Elissa to get over the loss of her husband.

In the pouring rain, it was impossible to see the driver's face inside the SUV. He or she was nothing more than a dark, blurry, human-shaped blob behind the wheel. But thanks to a fortuitous swipe of the Blazer's wiper blades at just the right moment, he did manage to get the license plate as the vehicle drove past. As the taillights faded down the access road and into the rain-swept night, Stone pulled over at the bottom of the Daggett driveway and radioed the plate information to Deputy Valentine back at the station.

He had his answer five minutes later. "Sheriff, that plate comes back to Steve Lepper."

"Copy that, thanks."

Stone sat for a few moments, kicking things around in his head, and something clicked in the back of his mind. He climbed out of the truck, feeling the rain pound against his Stetson and rancher's coat, and circled around to the back, where he found Milton Robbins's laptop buried under a pile of police gear. He hustled back to the cab, bringing the computer with him. He turned it on and saw there wasn't much battery life left, but hopefully it would be enough to get the job done.

No time to waste. He called Robbins.

The veteran answered on the fourth ring. "Hello?"

"Milt, it's Stone."

A long silence, then: "Uh, what can I do for you, preacher?"

"Actually, I'm calling you in my sheriff capacity. I need your help."

"Okaaaaay." Robbins drew the word out long and slow, making his hesitation clear. "Is this about the laptop I brought to you?"

"Indirectly, yeah. But it's really about something bigger."

"Am I in some kind of trouble?"

"Not at all," Stone replied. "I'm investigating a murder and I need the name of that amateur porn site you told me about, the one with Elissa Daggett on it."

"Is she in trouble?"

"I can't get into specifics, Milt. I just need the name of the site."

"I've been trying not to think about it, but if you think it will help…"

"It will."

A long sigh, and then Robbins said, "Okay. It's called mountainmount dot com."

Stone typed the address into the browser, immediately got a *This Site Is Age Restricted. Click Here To Confirm You Are Over 18* warning, and said, "Thanks, Milt. Sorry to bring up bad memories. I'll take it from here."

"If it'll help you, Sheriff, I can give you my login information. All of Elissa's videos are saved under my favorites on the site." The shame in Robbins' voice came through loud and clear.

"That would save me from having to dig around," Stone said. As Robbins rattled off the username and password, Stone accessed the website, clicked on the favorites section, and scrolled to the first video. The thumbnail image alone was X-rated. "Okay, Milt. I'm in."

"Anything else I can do for you?" Robbins asked.

"No, that's everything. Thanks for the help."

"No problem, preacher. God bless."

Stone felt like he needed God's blessing—and a shower—as he started to watch the videos. The first few were of Elissa and Preston engaging in some pretty basic married sexuality, with video quality that could best be described as low and amateurish. But as Stone continued to wade through the clips, the quality eventually improved, becoming much more high-definition, allowing the things being done on-screen to be seen even clearer. *Both a blessing and a curse*, Stone thought, as he continued to wade through the home-made pornography, looking for confirmation of what he suspected.

He found it on the thirteenth video.

This time, Elissa and Preston were joined by another man, and a classic threesome began to unfold. Some kind of editing software had been used to blur the other man's face into a jumbled mess of pixels, presumably to protect his identity.

But Stone didn't need to see his face to identify him.

The leprechaun tattoo on Steve Lepper's wrist did that just fine.

EIGHTEEN

STONE CLOSED THE LAPTOP, tossed it onto the passenger seat, and drove up the long driveway to the Daggett house. The porch was covered by a rustic awning and a bulb smeared yellow light on the front door. Stone moved hurriedly through the rain, took the steps two at a time, and rang the doorbell. He heard chimes from deep inside the house.

He pressed the button three more times before Elissa Daggett finally opened the door. She wore a barely closed bathrobe that exposed a generous amount of cleavage and leg, her hair wet, like she had just got out of the shower. She smelled like floral-scented shampoo or body wash. It reminded him of all the Bath & Body Works bottles his ex-wife had kept stacked in their shower before the death of their daughter tore their marriage apart.

"Catch you at a bad time?" Stone asked.

"With me, Sheriff, there's no such thing as a bad time." Elissa's smile let him know he could take that comment any way he wanted. "Come on in and tell me what I can do for you."

She turned and sauntered away, clearly expecting Stone to follow. He obliged and there was no doubt that she was giving her hips a little extra sway, like she was moving to the rhythm of some internal rock beat. Stone just shook his head. Yeah, this little lady was really trying to crank up the heat. Maybe being an ex-stripper, she just couldn't help giving men something to put their eyes on.

She led him into the living room and sat down in a recliner, crossing her legs with a wide, exaggerated motion that provided Stone with prolonged visual proof that there was nothing underneath the robe. He did his best to keep his eyes averted as she motioned at the sofa across from her. "Have a seat, Sheriff. Rest those aching bones of yours and take a load off, as they say."

"I'll stand, thanks."

Elissa shrugged. "Suit yourself. What's this about?"

"There's no easy way to say this."

"Is this about Preston?"

Stone nodded. "The deer didn't kill him."

"No?" Her eyes widened slightly. "Then how did he die?"

Stone decided to go with the direct approach. "He was murdered. Someone stabbed him and then impaled his body on the antlers to try to cover up the wound." He watched her closely to gauge her reaction.

"Oh my god!"

Stone's eyes narrowed. Her shocked reaction was appropriate, but her delivery seemed about as fake as her augmented breasts.

"Sorry for being so blunt," he said. "Just like ripping off a band-aid, sometimes it's best just to get the bad news out of the way."

She waved away his apology, her long fingernails painted bloodred. "No, I appreciate you not treating me gentle, like I'm some kind of delicate flower that can't handle the hard"—slight pause—"truth."

Stone continued to watch her. The shock, whether real or fake, looked like it was already wearing off.

"Do you have any suspects?" she asked.

"Right now, just one."

"Anybody I know?"

"Actually, you know him quite well," Stone replied. "How long have you been sleeping with Steve Lepper?"

Elissa didn't even try to deny it. She actually looked relieved more than anything else, as if happy she no longer needed to hide the affair. "How did you find out, if you don't mind me asking?" She didn't wait for an answer and immediately dismissed the question with a wave of her manicured hand. "Never mind, it doesn't matter."

Stone told her anyway. "If you want something to stay a secret, you probably shouldn't make videos and put them on the internet."

She nodded, drew in a deep breath, and then exhaled it long and slow. "It started out as a mutual experimentation thing, harmless enough, just Preston and I trying to spice things up in the bedroom, you know?"

"Actually," Stone said, "no, I don't."

Elissa waved another dismissive hand. "You're a preacher. Of course you know about boring sex."

Stone stayed silent, refusing to take the bait. No way in hell was he going down that road with her.

"Anyway," Elissa finally continued, "it eventually became something more."

"What do you mean by that?"

"Steve and I fell for each other," she replied. "What started as lust turned into love. That's the risk you take when you bring another person into your sex life. Sometimes they turn out to be a better fit than your spouse. Steve was opening a strip club, I wanted to dance again, and we had...other mutual interests...as well."

"Meaning?"

Elissa sighed. "Meaning Preston was a dull lay who didn't know the first thing about getting a woman off, and Steve knew every trick in the book."

"How did Preston feel about all that?"

"He forbade me from stripping ever again." Elissa snickered. "That's the actual word he used—forbade."

"I get it," Stone said dryly. "Educated men are such turnoffs."

"Don't judge me, Mr. Stone."

"That's God's job, not mine."

"Anyway, Preston shut down the threesomes. Said he didn't want to share me anymore." Elissa plucked a pack of cigarettes off the table next to her chair and fired one up, uncrossing and then recrossing her legs as she did so, slow and deliberate, offering Stone another eyeful of her nakedness. She blew smoke out of the corner of her mouth and smiled crookedly at him. "But we all remained friends."

"You know, that all sounds like a good motive for murder," said Stone, locking eyes with her. "Wife starts banging another guy, gets sick of the husband, and suddenly the husband is out of the way. Pretty convenient."

"You cannot seriously believe that I had anything to do with Preston's death." This time, her shock seemed genuine.

"You need to put on some clothes and come down to the station with me to answer some questions and get this all sorted out."

Elissa stared at him for several long seconds, then took a long drag on the cigarette that hollowed out her cheeks before she reached down and unknotted the sash holding her robe closed. "We should skip going to the station, Sheriff. I think we'd both be more comfortable right here." Both sides fell open, fully exposing her body. Preacher or not, sheriff or not, Stone was still a red-blooded male, and he readily admitted to himself that it was one hell of a body. God had been on point the day He put her together.

But that didn't change anything.

"Go put some clothes on, Elissa," he said.

"You've heard about girls who can suck a golf ball through a garden hose?" She exhaled the smoke and purred her words. "Well, I can do it with a bowling ball." She tossed a wink his way. "Think about the possibilities, Sheriff."

"Enough of this crap," Stone growled. He crossed the room in three large strides and slapped the cuffs on her, ratcheting them around her delicate wrists. "I'm guessing this isn't your first time wearing these."

"Oh, very kinky," she said. "Maybe you should call that pretty little waitress you've got a hard-on for and see if she wants to join us. I could teach you both a few things that'll make you think you found heaven on earth."

Stone closed her robe, retied the belt with a double knot to make sure it didn't come open again, and led her out to the Blazer. He didn't give a damn that she was getting rained on.

"Elissa Daggett, you're under arrest."

————

After turning Elissa over to Deputy Sanchez at the station, Stone headed up the street to the Jack Lumber Bar & Grill. The rain had reduced itself down to a light drizzle. He needed a drink—well, maybe *need* was too strong a word, but he definitely *wanted* a drink—and an ear to bend.

He found Grizzle behind the bar as usual. He swore the man slept there...if he slept at all. Well into his seventies, maybe the tough old codger had reached that stage of life where sleep was an option rather than a necessity. Stone's grandfather had been that way, needing little more than an occasional catnap to get by.

There were a few patrons scattered around the joint, including a young couple slow-dancing to an overplayed piano ballad by Extreme that, for some reason, made him think of Holly. But things were quiet enough that Grizzle was able to pay attention as Stone relayed the recent turn of events. Grizzle just listened quietly, occasionally nodding, the long scars on his face from the bear claws all those years ago looking bright and rubbery under the lights.

Not for the first time, Stone thought that the barkeeper had the face of a wise man, a sage, the kind of elder who had ridden the hard trail a time or two and learned more than a thing or two along the way. One thing was for sure—Grizzle was damn easy to talk to and could be trusted with secrets when spoken by a friend. Over his usual Jack and Coke, lots of ice, easy on the Jack, Stone brought him up to speed.

Grizzle was quiet for several moments, contemplative, and then gave Stone a crooked grin. "So what I'm getting out of all this is that Elissa Daggett is giving Holly some competition for your affections."

"You're such an ass," Stone said.

"Hey, I don't blame you, not one bit. Elissa is a very attractive woman."

"Don't make me hurt you, Griz."

"Gonna break poor Holly's heart, though, when she hears the news."

"I came here for advice, not wisecracks."

"Advice about the case or advice about Elissa?"

Stone rolled his eyes so hard he swore he saw the back of his skull. "The case, you damn fool."

"Aw, hell, that's easy," Grizzle said. "That itch you've been having? Like I told you before, just keep scratching it and you'll get that case solved."

"And like I said, sometimes you scratch too hard and shit starts to bleed."

Grizzle stroked his sparsely whiskered chin. "Pain is often easier to endure than an itch."

"You just make that up?"

"Nah, got it off a fortune cookie years ago." The barkeep grinned, then immediately sobered. "Listen, my friend, fact of the matter is, I suspect more blood's gonna get shed before you get to the bottom of this case."

"If that's what it takes, then so be it," Stone said.

Grizzle shook his head in bemused wonderment. "You may drink weak-ass whiskey, but you're one ice-cold bastard of a preacher."

"I'll take that as a compliment."

"Take it any way you like. What's your next move?"

"Already got Elissa Daggett behind bars, so now it's time to go round up Steve Lepper."

"You got the proof to keep 'em locked up?"

"Not yet, but I can hold them for seventy-two hours while I figure it out." Stone drained his weak-ass whiskey and slid off the barstool. "Thanks for the drink, Griz. And thanks for listening."

"Don't go doing anything stupid," Grizzle replied. "But get that itch scratched. Just don't go getting a bullet in your ass in the process."

"From your lips to God's ears," said Stone as he headed out the door.

———

Stone thought about waiting until the morning to round up Lepper, but he wasn't in a patient mood. He left the bar and drove straight to Lepper's house, a rustic A-frame built on a back road between the town of Bloomingdale and the hamlet of Gabriels, situated on a 70-acre plot of marshy woods that ensured no neighbors, lots of mosquitoes in the warm months, and plenty of privacy.

Stone pulled into the driveway and press-checked his Glock to confirm there was a round in the chamber. Part of him wanted to just put a bullet between Lepper's eyes and be done with the matter, and he might have done exactly that if he had definitive proof that Lepper murdered Preston Daggett. But right now all he had was suspicion, hardly enough to justify executing the man. Just because Lepper was screwing Elissa didn't automatically mean he had killed Preston.

He needed answers.

Stone studied the darkened windows. The porch light was off. It wasn't that late but maybe Lepper was one of those early-to-bed kind of guys. Or, hell, maybe he wasn't even home. Maybe he had somehow heard about Elissa's arrest and was already in the wind, leaving her holding the bag.

Or maybe he was sitting in the dark with a gun pointed at the door, just waiting for Stone to knock. If Lepper had already killed once, what was one more? Stone knew all too well that the first kill was the hardest. After that, the killing got a whole lot easier.

He climbed out of the Blazer and cautiously stepped up onto the porch. He didn't pull out his

Glock but kept it loose in the holster, ready for rapid acquisition. He could draw with rattlesnake-strike speed if the need arose. This far out in the boonies, nobody would even hear the shots if this attempted arrest spiraled out of control and into gunplay.

He thought about calling for backup, but quickly said the hell with it. He had spent a lot of years working alone in some of the most cutthroat places on earth and he was used to having nobody to rely on but himself. Most of the time, he preferred it that way.

Like right now.

Stone stepped to the side—any bullets that came through the door weren't going to find him standing there waiting for them—and knocked with the side of his fist, banging hard in case Lepper was asleep.

"Steve? It's Sheriff Stone. Need you to come to the door."

Nothing stirred inside. At least, nothing that Stone could hear. As far as he knew, Lepper lived alone, with no wife, no kids, not even a dog.

He banged on the door again. "Steve! It's Sheriff Stone. Open up."

Nothing but silence.

"Hell with this," Stone growled. He drew his Glock with his right hand, grabbed his flashlight with his left, and kicked in the door.

He immediately spun back behind cover as the door flew open with a splintered cracking sound. After a long, slow ten-count during which no bullets came buzzing out at him, he edged through the breached doorway and thumbed on his flashlight. The powerful beam chased away the darkness.

In the harsh, scouring glare of the light, he saw Lepper sitting silently on the couch.

Silent because someone had blown his face off with a shotgun.

Stone took a long, hard look at the shredded mess of pulped flesh and shattered bone and sighed.

"Well, shit."

NINETEEN

TO MAKE up for running out on their dinner, Stone met Holly for breakfast at the diner early the next morning. For once, she was there before him, which was proof that miracles still happened. He tossed back the first cup of coffee like a college coed doing a tequila shot, before their waitress could even walk away with the pot. She raised her eyebrows and immediately poured him another cup. This one he drank more slowly, silently urging the caffeine to inject itself into his bloodstream and chase away the drowsiness. He had slept like crap last night and the shower this morning hadn't helped much.

"You look a little better than roadkill, but not by much," Holly said. "Rough night?"

"You could say that."

"You have a bad one-night stand or something?"

"You jealous?"

She smirked. "Who says I didn't have one of my own?"

Stone grinned. "Well played. I deserved that."

"Yeah, you did." Holly switched subjects. "So is it true what they're saying? That Steve Lepper and Elissa Daggett were having an affair and now somebody killed Lepper?"

"Damn." Stone shook his head. "I might never get used to how fast news travels around here."

"It's a small town," Holly replied. "That's the way it works." She jerked a thumb over her shoulder at the waitress. "Megan overheard some of the early birds talking about it and filled me in while I waited for you to show up. So it's true?"

"Yeah, it's true."

She started to say something, but her cell phone buzzed, interrupting her train of thought. She glanced at the number and Stone saw the blood drain from her face. Even a ghost would have said she looked pale.

He reached for her across the table. "Holly, are you—"

She held up a finger in a *wait-a-minute* gesture and answered the phone. "Hello?"

Stone felt his guts churning, his veins turning cold. Something wasn't right.

"Wait...what? How did this happen?" Pause. "How long before they get here?" Pause. "Yes, I understand. I'll find somewhere safe. At this point, I'll do a better job protecting me and Lizzy than you are. Hell, you guys couldn't even protect your own man." Pause. "Yeah, I'm sure you're sorry about all this. Maybe you can tell everybody how sorry you are at our funerals."

She angrily hit the button on her phone to hang up,

stabbing it with enough force that Stone worried she might crack the screen.

"What was that all about?" he asked.

She didn't say anything.

"Holly, talk to me."

She clutched the phone and stared out the window, lips pursed in silence, her face a mask of fear and anger. Finally she turned to him and said, "That was the US Marshal Service. My handler, Cade Rogers, was murdered last night, along with his wife and son and their nanny. They're pretty sure my ex-husband did it, and they think he knows my new name and how to find me and Lizzy." A single tear slid down her cheek and she hastily brushed it away as if offended by the sign of weakness. "They think he's on his way here."

"Are you serious?"

Holly nodded. "Dead serious." She brayed a harsh, half-hysterical laugh. "No pun intended on the 'dead' part." She took a deep breath and seemed to pull herself together. "They told me to get Lizzy and hole up in the safest place I can think of until they send a protection detail."

"Did they say how long that will take?"

"They weren't sure."

"Unacceptable," Stone said. "You and Lizzy will stay at my place until this shit gets sorted out."

"Your place? Really?"

"Damn straight. Until the dust settles, I'll be your protection detail."

"At this stage of the game, I definitely trust you more than them."

"Does this mean they'll relocate you?" Stone tried to ignore how much that thought hurt his heart.

"I...I don't know," Holly replied. "Maybe. I don't want to go, but I'm not sure I have a choice, and I've got Lizzy to think about. I absolutely cannot let her father get his filthy hands on her."

"That son of a bitch will have to go through me first," Stone rasped. "I'll put a bullet in his heart and not even ask God for forgiveness because I'd be doing His work."

She smiled at that. "I'm still not sure you've gotten the hang of this whole preacher thing."

"I'll keep working on it," Stone replied. "First things first, we need to get you and Lizzy out to my place ASAP."

"People are going to talk, Luke." Holly looked worried. "Half the town already doesn't believe we're just friends, and now it'll look like we're shacking up. Like I said before, this is a small town, and gossip spreads like wildfire around here."

"In case you haven't figured it out by now, I don't give a damn what people say. What I give a damn about is you and Lizzy. People can think whatever they want."

Holly started texting on her phone. "I'm letting Lizzy know to come to your house after school."

"You telling her Jack might be on his way here?"

Holly shook her head. "No, I don't want to break the bad news to her by text. I'll tell her tonight." She suddenly looked worried. "She'll be safe at school, right?"

"Should be. We can go pull her out early if you want."

"No, it's fine."

They quickly finished their breakfast and then drove out to Holly's house so she could grab some things for her and Lizzy. Stone carried the bags out to the truck and then they headed to his place. Max greeted them at the door with a quick sniff and wag of his tail, then flopped down on his dog bed with a heavy sigh as if to say, *You guys seem amped up. I'm gonna take a nap 'til you calm down.*

Stone immediately went down into the basement and got his guns out of the vault. If Jack Dawson came calling with hostile intent, Stone wanted more than his duty-carry Glock to deal with the situation.

The Heckler & Koch UMP-45 submachine gun and Smith & Wesson Stealth Hunter Performance .44 Magnum revolver would do nicely for starters. He carried them over to the bar area built into the corner of the room and laid them out. He checked and double-checked their actions and then made sure both weapons were fully loaded. He went back to the vault and took out the HK416 carbine and the Seekins Precision Havak Pro rifle, chambered for a .338 WinMag round in case he needed longer-range options.

"You look like you're preparing for war," Holly remarked, coming down the stairs to check on him.

"Let's hope not," he said, sliding the bolt forward on the Seekins.

"Thanks for taking us in, Luke. Between Max and Rocky"—she was referring to the abused horse he had rescued earlier in the year—"you're really getting good at picking up strays." She smiled at him. "You might be some kind of badass, Bible-thumping gunslinger, but you've got a heart bigger than Texas."

Stone shrugged. "I've done a lot of bad things in my life. Guess sometimes I just try to balance the scales."

"But all those bad things you did, they were for good reasons, right?"

Another shrug. "I thought so at the time." *And I haven't stopped doing bad things for good reasons*, he silently added. *Just like I'll kill Jack Dawson in cold blood if that's what it takes.*

In the woods behind the high school, the scent of blood hung in the air.

But this time, it wasn't Lizzy doing the bleeding.

This time, the blood belonged to the Macero twins, and neither sister seemed happy to have the tables turned on them.

Nova sat tangled up in the exposed roots of a large birch tree, cramming tissues up her crushed nostrils to stop the flow of blood. Her red-rimmed eyes leaked tears and she looked absolutely miserable. Lizzy had knocked her scrawny ass to the ground with three hard punches.

Seeing her sister felled by Lizzy's fists, Petra had done what most bullies do when their victim fights back—retreated like a coward. She scrambled back-ward, the cruel predator now hunted by the no-longer-helpless prey. The wolves were learning that, when pushed hard enough, the sheep will kick back.

Luke was right, Lizzy thought. *Bullies really don't like it when you stand up for yourself.*

Frozen leaves and brittle pine needles crunched underfoot as she stalked toward Petra. The girl turned to Lizzy and raised her fists to defend herself, but looked scared, vulnerable, and woefully uncertain about this unexpected turn of events.

"Stop! Please!" Petra cried out. Her voice trembled and it didn't sound like she was faking her distress. "Please, Lizzy. I'm begging you, just leave me and my sister alone."

"I begged, and you didn't listen," Lizzy snapped. "Now you reap what you sowed."

"Nova is hurt," Petra said. "Look at her—you broke her nose! What's done is done. You made your point."

"I'll decide when the point's been made."

Lizzy kept moving forward, closing in. She didn't necessarily want to beat the girls to a pulp, but she needed to make enough of a statement to make sure they never messed with her again. One broken nose wasn't sufficient to get that message across.

Petra launched a wild, desperate punch. Lizzy easily dodged it, pivoted on her heel, and fired a kick into the meat of the girl's thigh. Petra's leg buckled, dropping her to one knee. As she went down, Lizzy swung a looping overhand strike and felt her knuckles crack against Petra's cheekbone. Her head whipped to the side as she went sprawling across the ground in a flurry of dirt, dust, and decayed leaves.

Looks like Luke's lessons really paid off.

Petra crawled over to her sister and they both leaned against the tree roots, huddled side by side, staring up at Lizzy with expressions of fear and loathing. The tissues that had been white when Nova tucked them into her nostrils were now bright red. Lizzy's punch had split the skin over Petra's cheekbone and blood streaked down her face. She swiped a hand at it, smearing it across her jaw like smudged war paint.

"How's it feel to be on the other side of a beating?" Lizzy snapped.

"Please just stop." Petra started to cry, snot bubbling down over her upper lip. Her breath came in short, sharp gasps as if she was suffocating, unable to draw enough oxygen into her lungs.

Lizzy stared down at her, heart beating like a metronome. Her pulse throbbed with savagery, a burning need to hurt her enemy even more, maybe even break a bone or two. Petra's pain, panic, and pleading were like a primal elixir setting her blood on fire.

But cutting just beneath the surface of that primeval pull was an undercurrent of anxiety, the knowledge that she needed to pull back and not surrender to her violent impulses with reckless abandon, without control. Lizzy knew she had proved her point, made it crystal clear that she was not someone to be fucked with. Further bloodshed would be unjustified brutality for brutality's sake, a slaking of the lizard brain's thirst for carnage and payback, and she didn't want to descend to that level.

Rise above, she told herself. *Be better than that.*

She took three long breaths, followed by equally long exhalations, and by the time she was done, the rage had somewhat receded. It was still there, hot embers in the background, but no longer an all-consuming fire.

Nova groaned, gingerly touching her busted nose, which was swelled to twice its normal size. "Fucking hell," she muttered.

Petra seemed to realize the immediate threat was over, that Lizzy wasn't going to stomp them into bloody piles of roadkill like they deserved, and her bluster came surging back. "We're gonna call the cops on you, bitch!"

Lizzy's lips peeled back from her teeth in a cold, bemused grin. "Go right ahead."

"Don't act like you want us to call the pigs. That reverse psychology crap won't work on us, you little tramp."

"The sheriff is practically my stepdad these days," Lizzy retorted. "For that matter, he's the one who told me to stand up to you two bitches and taught me the moves to do it. Hell, my mom texted me and said we're staying at his house tonight for some reason, so I'll save you the phone call and just let him know about this beat down over supper tonight."

"This ain't over. Not by a long shot," Petra seethed. Both twins climbed to their feet but made no move to attack, settling for harsh threats instead. "You hear me, Liz-bo? Payback's coming and it's gonna be a real bitch. You won't know what hit you."

"Like I said, I'll be at Sheriff Stone's place. So if you want a rematch, you know where to find me."

The twins slinked away and Lizzy watched them go, relishing the fact that she had finally gotten the upper hand. She felt confident, avenged, like the pieces of her life were fitting back into place after the havoc Petra and Nova had wrought. She wondered if the two sisters would tell anyone about what had happened, but didn't really give a shit one way or the other. Her classmates had known she was being bullied by the Maceros and turned a blind eye. She had zero doubt they would just as readily turn a blind eye to the Maceros getting what they had coming to them.

She headed off to school, smiling for what felt like the first time in forever.

Nothing like beating up some bullies to start the day off right.

TWENTY

JACK DAWSON AVOIDED the highways and used the back roads from Cranberry Lake, Long Lake, and Tupper Lake to slip into Whisper Falls under cover of darkness, long after the sidewalks had been rolled up and the only places open for business were the bars and late-night pizza joints. The only person he passed on the sidewalk was a drunk vomiting into a trash can and muttering, "Goddamned chicken wings."

Dawson strolled into the Nailed Coffin nonchalantly, acting like he owned the shithole, and ordered a beer that was handed to him by a bartender who clearly didn't like strangers in his saloon. The term "hairy eyeball" had been invented to describe the look the barkeep was giving him. Not that Dawson gave a damn. He ignored the hostile stare and leaned on the bar with one elbow as he surveyed the joint.

To borrow a phrase from *Road House*, it looked like

the kind of place you had to sweep the eyeballs off the floor at the end of the night.

You're a hell of a long way from Vegas, Jack.

Still, whatever it took to find Holly, though he still had a hard time thinking about her with that name.

He scanned the bar, wondering if any of the local-yokels would be willing to cough up the information he needed. He could always come back here with his boys and strongarm somebody for the intel—amazing what somebody will say with a gun to their groin—but he wanted to keep a lower profile than that.

There was a rowdy crew wearing the name-patched, grease-stained uniforms from what he presumed was a local automotive garage, whooping it up over in the corner booth and generally acting like they were ready to raise some hell. The fact that they were all still in their work clothes at this time of night indicated they had hit the bar right after their shift and never left. Which meant they had probably done a lot of drinking and wouldn't be hard to deal with if it came down to a fight.

There was a guitar player set up on a small stage at the back of the joint, strumming acoustic covers of '70s and '80s rock songs, but nobody was paying him much attention because he played like crap and sang even worse. He was currently murdering his way through a truly awful rendition of "Freebird." Dawson hated that overhyped, overplayed tune.

At the other end of the bar stood a trio of guys engaged in low conversation. From the snippets that Dawson managed to overhear, it sounded like they were talking about a bootleg poker game going on in some back room. He took a swig of beer and idly wondered if any of the players had gone up against a professional card shark like himself. Seemed unlikely in a town that most likely had more cow chips than poker chips.

Dawson avoided direct eye contact with anyone, even the ones who tried to stare him down. The last thing he needed right now was a tussle that would bring the cops running. Even hick-town huckleberry badge-wearers like the ones that no doubt jackbooted around this pathetic little town would not take long to figure out that he was a wanted man. There was even a medium security federal prison—FCI Ray Brook— just ten miles away that they could drag him to until the marshals came to collect, classify him as a high-level escape risk, and toss his ass into solitary confinement for the rest of his life.

The door opened and Dawson stopped thinking about prison as he found himself staring into a pair of gorgeous green eyes framed by a pair of black plastic glasses that looked like they belonged on a librarian. The eyes—and the glasses—belonged to the attractive woman now giving him an appraising, appreciative glance. Dark-blonde hair held neatly in place, a little makeup that attempted to hide her middle-age truth, a quirky smile that showcased a tiny dimple, and breasts that nicely filled out the blouse beneath her open jacket.

If she can't help me find my ex-wife, Dawson thought, *she could probably at least help me forget about her for a while. A body like that could keep a man going all night long.*

The woman blinked a few times, studying him with frank openness, and then moved to the bar, standing a few feet away from him as she ordered a Long Island Iced Tea.

Such a girly drink, Dawson thought, then cleared his throat and said, "I'd be happy to buy that drink for you if you could help me find a relative of mine. We lost touch years ago, but I heard she moved to these parts recently."

"Doubt I would know her," the woman replied as the bartender dropped a cocktail napkin in front of her and set the glass on top.

"How can you be sure? I haven't even told you her name yet."

"I make it a point to stay out of other people's business." The woman smiled at him. "You still gonna buy me this drink?"

Dawson's first instinct was to grab the bitch by the throat, sink his fingers into her esophagus, and choke the fucking information out of her. But he managed to rein in his anger. "Minding your own business is a good life philosophy," he said. "But really, I'm just looking for my cousin, Holly Bennett. Any chance you've heard of her?"

"Can't say I have."

"Can't…or won't?"

"Listen, don't go turning into a jerk now, stud. I haven't heard of her and that's all there is to it. Don't go reading into it, and don't make something out of nothing."

"Sorry, you're right." Dawson dropped some bills, stolen from Cade Rogers's wallet after he shot him in the mouth, on the bar. "The drink's on me. Enjoy." *And I hope you choke on it, you bitch.*

"Well, that's right sweet of you." She tapped her fingers to the rhythm of the music—if you could call it that—coming from the stage. The guy was currently murdering a Motley Crue song. "What do you think of the guitar player?" she asked.

"Honestly? I think he sounds like shit."

The woman snapped her head around fast enough to risk whiplash and glared at him. "Excuse me? That's my boyfriend, I'll have you know."

"Sorry."

Her eyes narrowed behind the glasses. "Sorry for what? Sorry for what you said, or sorry that he's my boyfriend?"

"Let's just say that I hope he treats you better than he's treating that guitar."

The woman raised her voice, drawing the attention Dawson had wanted to avoid. "First you practically rape me with your eyes—or *eye*, I should say, since you're playing pirate tonight—and then you start pestering me for information about a local, and then you insult my boyfriend and start hitting on me? Are you for real, mister?"

All eyes in the bar were on them now.

Shit.

"Listen, you've got it all wrong," Dawson said, trying to smooth things over before the situation got fucked seven ways from Sunday. "This is all just a big misunderstanding. Let me buy you another drink, top shelf, to apologize for the trouble."

The music had stopped mid-chord, making it real

damn easy for everyone to hear the argument going down. The guitarist stomped off the stage and stormed over to Dawson, getting right up in his grill, completely unaware that he was nose-to-nose with one of the most dangerous men in America. "What the hell, dipshit? You hitting on my girl? Listen, punk, if you're looking for trouble, you came to the right place in the right town on the right night."

The mechanics in the corner booth were now on their feet, looking unhappy, looking like they were ready to put their boots to work stomping the snot out the stranger who had made the mistake of wandering into their watering hole. The three men at the other end of the bar moved closer, one of them cracking his knuckles as if warming up his fists. Dawson cursed himself for telling his men to stay out of town. He could really use some backup right about now.

But maybe he could defuse the situation with words before it came to blows. "Whoa, whoa, whoa," he said. "Hold on for just a second. Sorry if your girl got the impression I was making a move on her. I assure you, not my intention at all. I'm just looking for information about my cousin who moved here a few years back. If anybody here can point me in the direction of Holly Bennett, I'll be happy to pay you for your time and be on my way."

"So you want us to help you stalk some other chick?" The guitarist sneered. "Seriously, dude, what the hell?"

"Like I said, she's my cousin, and she owes me money. Just trying to track her down and collect what's owed me. Rolled into town, heard the music, figured I would grab a beer and maybe see if some-body can help me out."

"What you wanted to grab was my girl's ass," the guitarist snapped. "And what you want help with is getting your dick wet."

"You've got it all wrong," Dawson said.

"Fuck him up, Gary!" one of the mechanics yelled. "Don't let this pirate wannabe fancy-talk you out of defending your girl's honor!"

One-on-one, Dawson knew he could destroy Gary the Guitarist in about three-point-five seconds flat. But things would get a whole lot more dicey when—not if —the others ganged up to take him down. Didn't matter who was right and who was wrong, the mob would defend one of their own against an outsider. And a fight that resulted in a hospital visit and-slash-or the cops getting called was a one-way ticket back to the world of razor wire, guard towers, and iron bars. He could not let this situation erupt into violence. De-escalation remained his only viable course of action.

"Look," he said, holding up his hands, palms out. "I absolutely did not come here looking for a fight."

"No," Gary retorted. "You came here looking for some mystery woman that nobody seems to know." He reached over, grabbed the green-eyed lady's arm just above the elbow, and pulled her away. "You need to just mind your own business, asshole, and stop hitting on women who are already taken."

Dawson didn't bother correcting him again and the tension fizzled out of the air like a slow-leaking balloon. The men heckled the guitarist for being a sissy while simultaneously keeping an eye on the stranger in their midst, no doubt subconsciously sensing something dangerous about Dawson. They puffed themselves up with false bravado and told themselves they could have taken him, but he could read the uncertainty in their worried eyes.

Gary guided his girl to an empty booth and left her nursing the drink that Dawson had paid for, then jumped back up on the stage. "Sorry about the interruption," he said, slinging the guitar back over his shoulder and speaking into the cheap microphone with a squealing burst of feedback. "Now, who's ready for some more music?"

"Is that what you were playing before...music? I couldn't tell!" one of the mechanics called out. His booze-buddies whooped and hollered their encouragement, slapping their denim-clad thighs like it was the best damn joke they had ever heard.

"Ya'll a bunch of funny fuckers." Gary grinned good-naturedly and launched into a godawful rendition of Poison's "Nothing But A Good Time," which in his hands turned out to be anything but a good time. He only hummed the verse but sang the chorus, and it sounded like he was choking on a chicken bone while simultaneously gargling broken glass and washing it all down with battery acid.

As the music-slash-caterwauling kicked back into gear, Dawson cruised around the bar flashing a large wad of green, making it clear he was willing to pay for information about Holly Bennett. Nobody took him up on the offer, but somehow, word must have reached the poker game in the back room because a short time later, a man appeared from the back regions of the bar and approached. The guy was an ex-con, no doubt about it. Dawson recognized one of his own.

"Who the fuck are you?" the man asked without preamble.

"I could ask you the same thing," Dawson replied.

"I'm Vance Macero. Now you know my name. Let's have yours."

"No offense, but I'd rather not give it."

"Mr. Mysterious, huh?" Macero raked him with his steely gaze. "Fine, keep that shit to yourself for all I care. You looking for a few rounds of Texas Hold 'Em? Word's getting around that you've got the greenbacks for it."

"I don't have time for a game," Dawson said. He held up the wad of cash. "But maybe you can play in my place."

Macero eyeballed the money and licked his cracked lips greedily. "Maybe. Depends on what I've gotta do for the bankroll. Heard you're looking for some woman."

"Holly Bennett. You know where she lives?"

"Sure do, but she and that brat of hers ain't there."

"Then where are they?"

"If I tell you, every last dollar of that money in your hand is mine."

"Deal. But if your information turns out to be bull-shit, I'm coming back here for my money and your life."

Macero snickered. "You better bring friends, pal."

"I've got friends that will tear through this place and everyone in it like a Kansas tornado," Dawson said. "Now, tell me where I can find Holly Bennett and her daughter."

"They're at the preacher's house. Or the sheriff's house, I should say."

"Well, which is it?"

"It's the same place. The preacher is also the sheriff."

"Strange, but whatever. Give me his name, his address, sketch me a map, and the money is all yours."

"His name is Lucas Stone." Macero plucked a napkin from a dispenser on the bar and jotted down the address along with a crude, hastily drawn map. "There ya go."

"Much obliged." Dawson handed over the money. "Good luck with the cards."

"Need you to do me one favor," Macero said.

"And what would that be?"

"Stone gives you any trouble, make him sorry he was ever born."

Dawson smiled. "That's the plan, my friend."

TWENTY-ONE

STONE LAY in bed with the Smith & Wesson Stealth Hunter Performance .44 Magnum revolver within easy reach on the nightstand, along with a speed loader bristling with extra cartridges. Outside, a harvest moon glowed in the heavens like a blood orange, somehow both beautiful and sinister at the same time. He had tracked its celestial journey across the night sky since he had not slept a single, solitary wink. Dawn was still hours away, but Stone knew there would be no sleep for him that night.

He hoped Holly and Lizzy, tucked into the guest bedrooms at the other end of the house, were faring better than he was. Max was curled up in the hallway between their rooms as if sensing they were here for protection and doing his doggy-damnedest to provide it. If anybody wanted to hurt them, they would have to get through the Shottie's powerful jaws to do it.

Stone stared at the ceiling, at the overhead fan above the bed, trying to let the low, thrumming oscillation of the wooden blades hypnotize him to sleep. But his brain was too keyed up, too activated, too *switched on* to permit any semblance of slumber.

And then there was the voice of guilt, the nagging, serpentine hiss that kept reminding him that he had become a preacher to atone for the violence of his past, yet somehow kept finding himself neck-deep in more violence. A voice that constantly asked him if a man of faith could also be—or rather, *should* be—a man of the gun.

It was a hard voice to silence. Especially lying in bed with a .44 Magnum hand cannon next to him.

He let the doubts and questions swirl around in his head without even trying to figure out any answers, let alone the right ones. If there were even any right ones to be found. The dead of night was prime time for soul-searching, but the answers you found under the cover of darkness often didn't look so good in the light of dawn.

Regardless of the right or wrong of it, he knew he would do whatever it took to protect Holly and Lizzy from the dangerous clutches of Jack Dawson. If the son of a bitch came here looking for them, Stone had zero intention of letting him walk away with his life. There would be no arrest, no handcuffs, no indictment, no defense attorney, no trial…none of that shit.

There would only be execution.

Cold, hard, primal justice.

Another sleepless hour rolled by, the moon dragging itself across the sky, the house silent save for the occasional muted hum of the furnace kicking on down in the basement. Stone could not shake his restlessness. He was going to need lots of coffee in the morning. He could not afford to be lethargic if Dawson came calling.

His bedroom door crept open with a soft creak, a brass hinge protesting its lack of oil.

Stone's hand automatically reached for the revolver, but a half-heartbeat later, he recognized the shape of the shadow slipping into his room. "Holly?" he said softly.

"It's me," she responded, as if that explained everything, when in fact it explained nothing. At least not as far as Stone was concerned. She pulled back the covers and slid into bed next to him. Not touching, not yet at least, but close enough that he could feel the heat coming off her skin.

"What are you doing?"

"I can't sleep and...and I don't want to be alone tonight." Her voice was barely a whisper in the darkness.

"Holly, I'm not sure this is a good idea."

Stone's heart hammered in his chest and his blood felt on fire. Physically, he wanted exactly what she was offering. But there was an unspoken agreement between them to not take things to this level, to remain rooted in the safety of friendship. They both carried emotional baggage, scars on their hearts, that made anything more than being friends the equivalent of trying to navigate a minefield. Sure, they both knew there was desire and attraction between them, but until this moment, neither of them had so much as voiced it, let alone acted on it.

"You're right, it might not be a good idea," Holly

replied softly. "But it's what I want. Jack is out there, hunting us, which means I could very well be dead soon." She paused for a moment, and when she spoke again, there was a hitch in her voice. "Luke, I don't want to die wondering what could have been between us."

"You're not going to die," Stone said, his voice low and fierce and tender. "Not while I'm here."

She moved to him, the soft sheets rippling over her scantily clad body. Despite his reservations, Stone couldn't bring himself to stop as she crawled on top of him and kissed him deeply. God, he wanted her so bad. The press of her lips, the taste of her tongue, her flesh sliding in satin friction against his...it all felt so right and so wrong at the same time, two warring emotions occupying a single heartbeat.

Don't do this! his brain screamed at him. *There's no turning back, no repairing the damage done.*

But his heart wasn't listening. Right now, the cost didn't matter.

The kiss deepened as they took from each other hungrily, burning, devouring, yielding to the months of unspoken want and need. He pulled her close, felt the warm press of her breasts against his shirtless chest. She moaned into his mouth as his hands roamed, sliding over her trembling flesh.

Holly broke the kiss just long enough to pull her nightgown over her head and cast it aside. It landed on the floor in a puddle of silken fabric. The orange glow of the moon bathed her naked body. Stone's hands responded to the invitation, stroking, teasing, making her gasp with need and hunger. She groaned as she writhed against him, feeling the hard, relentless manifestation of his own desire.

Stone closed his eyes and savored the sensations. It had been so damn long and he wanted her so damn bad.

But no.

Not like this.

"Holly." He reached up, put his hands on her shoulders, and gently pushed her away. "Holly, I'm sorry."

Her eyes were wide in the dark as he gently rolled her onto her side next to him. "Luke, what is it? What's wrong?"

"It's not right."

"It *feels* right."

"What you're feeling is fear," Stone said. "You're afraid you might die tomorrow and you want to feel alive one more time before that happens."

"Even if that's true, so what? What's wrong with us being together on what might be the final night of our lives?"

He turned toward her, propping himself up on one elbow. She looked stunning in the shadows of the room, still breathing heavily from their few moments of misplaced passion. "I don't want you to be with me just because you're afraid of dying," he said.

"That's not the only reason," she protested, but she said it quickly, maybe too quickly, as if trying to convince herself that she was telling the truth.

"Let me ask you this," Stone said. "If Jack hadn't escaped from prison and come looking for you, would you still be in my bed right now?"

"I...don't know."

Stone leaned over and brushed his lips against hers, just the faintest ghost of a kiss. "If and when the time comes for us to be more than friends," he said, "I don't want there to be *any* other reason."

She looked into his eyes for several long moments, then smiled with both understanding and sadness and pulled the covers up over her breasts. "You're right, of course. Maybe some night, but not tonight." She sighed. "You're a good man, Lucas Stone. But sometimes I wish you weren't."

He chuckled. "Sorry."

"Don't be sorry. It's just who you are, and one of the many reasons I lo—" Her voice caught. "Uh, like you." She started to climb out of bed.

"Going somewhere?" Stone asked.

"Back to my room."

"You can stay with me if you don't want to be alone."

"Are you sure?"

"Yeah, I'm sure."

Without hesitation, she slid back under the covers and curled up against him. This time, there was nothing sexual about it. She was just a hurting soul looking for comfort and Stone was happy to give it.

Later, the room still dark, she asked, "What does this mean for us?"

"I don't know," Stone answered honestly. "But I promise you that we'll talk about it down the road."

"Once Jack is out of the picture, you mean."

"That's what you want, right?"

"I want him dead," Holly hissed with surprising

savagery. The last time Stone had heard that much venom in her voice was when a narco-queen kidnapped Lizzy. "I want you to kill him."

Stone reached over and brushed his knuckles against her cheek. "If he comes here, it'll be his last stop before hell, I promise you that."

"You always know just what to say to make me feel better," Holly said. As if to prove the point, she was asleep just moments later.

Stone spent the rest of the night listening to her quiet breathing, staring at the ceiling, and trying to sort out the conflicted emotions in his head and heart.

TWENTY-TWO

USING Vance Macero's connections to the Garrison County criminal element, Dawson had managed to gather a ragtag army ready to wage war against Stone for the promise of substantial payouts once Holly and Lizzy were back in his clutches. Once the redneck dirt-bags—for that was how Dawson thought of them—had realized he was a mob boss with the kind of deep pockets they could only dream of, their greed had kicked into overdrive. They had gladly grabbed their guns and pledged mercenary allegiance to his cause.

Dawson and his pack of cutthroats gathered on the rarely used gravel road that cut through the state land at the back of Stone's property. Dawn was just a smoky smudge, the mountains silhouetted against the slowly graying sky. No traffic back here, no sounds of civilization, and it was still too early for birdsong. The chickadees would start their morning serenades soon, the crows would start cawing, and the wild turkeys would cut loose with their thundering gobbles. But for now, there was nothing but silence.

The calm before the coming firestorm.

The makeshift army was restless, ready for action. Their weapons were an assorted mix of AR-15s—some illegally modified for full-auto operation—along with shotguns, pistols, and hunting rifles. One tweaker who seemed to be coked right out of his fucking gourd sported a pair of Micro Uzis and wore denim-on-denim like Chuck Norris in *Invasion U.S.A.*

The three hardcases who had broken Dawson out of prison—and Dawson himself—carried FN SCAR assault rifles they had secured from a black-market dealer in northern Pennsylvania before crossing the border into New York down by Binghamton. The SCARs were used but well-maintained and would get the job done.

"From what I'm hearing, this Stone fella ain't gonna go down easy," the hardcase named Henry said. "He's taken out some real mean motherfuckers since he rolled into town a couple years ago. They say if he puts you in his crosshairs, he'll just rip the life right out of you, no mercy."

"Not sure that's how preachers are supposed to act, but whatever," Dawson replied. "We recon the house yet?"

"Just him, your ex-wife, and your daughter. A small stable out back with one horse in it, and apparently there's some kind of dog."

"Horse isn't hurting anything, so leave it alone. The dog goes down if it shows so much as a half-inch of fang. The preacher meets his maker even if he walks out buck naked with his hands raised high in surrender. Holly and Lizzy—" He just could not get used to those stupid names—"better not have so much as a scratch on them when this is over, or so help me God, I will execute the person who did it. Make sure the redneck brigade is clear on that point. We're rolling out in five minutes."

"There's still time to call this off," Henry cautioned. "We do this, there's no turning back. The feds will know this was you and pick up your trail. You could very well get your wife and kid back but end up right back in prison before you have a chance to say much more than hello."

"We're getting them back and that's all there is to it," Dawson replied. "I'm going to pay that bitch back for betraying me. A little vengeance to soothe the soul, you might say. In our world, you let a traitor live, you're finished, done, washed up. You'll never be seen as anything other than weak and pathetic. That's why that goddamned whore needs to die, slowly, by my hand. I'm going to make her suffer in ways she can't even begin to imagine."

"What about your kid?" Henry asked.

"I haven't decided what I'm going to do with her yet." None of Dawson's men knew that he had tried to sexually abuse his daughter when she was just five years old. That incident was the reason his wife had betrayed him to the feds. "I'll figure it out once I have her back."

"We'll make it happen, boss. The preacher or sheriff or whatever the fuck he is, he's still just one man. We'll destroy him. The chopper going to show up to haul our asses outta there once we snatch your wife and kid?"

"My man is reliable. He owes me a favor from way back, so he'll be there," Dawson said. "You just take care of that damn preacher. I want him sucking on the devil's cock before you can see the sun over the mountains."

One of the rednecks standing nearby overheard the comment and muttered, "All I want is enough money to get me the fuck outta this shit-hole town."

Dawson gave him the kind of look he usually reserved for cockroaches. "You live in a hell of your own making. Same as everyone else. And there isn't any savior coming to pull your ass out. You have to do it yourself."

"Hell is what we're gonna get when we lock horns with that damn preacher," the redneck retorted. "All sorts of rumors floatin' 'round town 'bout him being some kind of badass, top secret gov'ment soldier back in the day."

Dawson's look grew even more disgusted. "Find your balls, man. I don't put much stock in stupid rumors, especially when they're coming from a bunch of backwoods pissants."

The redneck slunk away, his voice carrying back through the early-dawn shadows. "Fuck you, Vegas boy. I ain't scared. Just sayin' what I heard, is all."

Dawson shook his head. Unbelievable that his life had come to this. He had once commanded legions of mobsters, now he was forced to work with lowlifes and tweakers who probably had more meth in their veins than courage.

Still, when you were fighting a war, you took any soldier you could find. An escaped convict couldn't afford to be choosy about who took up arms on his behalf.

Besides, every army needed cannon fodder and Dawson didn't give a damn how many people died to get him what he wanted.

He glanced up at the sky again, the earthy smell of the marsh next to the gravel road thick in his nostrils. It would be light soon, the ashen hint of dawn becoming ever brighter.

Time to strike.

———

Sometime before dawn, Holly slipped out of Stone's room so that Lizzy wouldn't catch them in bed together. Neither of them was ready to face the kinds of questions she would ask.

Now, none of them able to sleep, they all sat at the kitchen table drinking coffee to combat the effects of not getting much rest. Stone was the most alert since he was the one with the most experience at dealing with stressful situations with little shuteye. The Smith & Wesson .44 Magnum sat on the table next to his mug. The steam rising from the cup of java reminded him of gun smoke.

Holly kept glancing at the revolver and finally slid her gaze up to his face. "I can't help but feel like we're putting you in danger by being here."

"That asshole is putting himself in danger if he decides to show up here," Stone growled.

Holly smiled, but it was weak around the edges. "Tough guy talk is cool and all, but it won't stop a bullet."

"The only thing that's going to stop a bullet is your ex-husband's face."

Lizzy had been staring down into her cup of coffee as if it held the answers to the mysteries of the world. But at Stone's words, her head snapped up and she looked stricken. "Are you really going to kill my dad?"

Stone immediately regretted his harsh statement. *Way to go, idiot.* But he had always played it straight with the teenager and he wasn't going to stop now. He looked her in the eye and quietly asked, "How do you think this ends?"

Holly reached over and put a hand on her daughter's arm. "Lizzy, honey, the only way he's your father is biologically, not in any way that matters."

"Doesn't change the fact that he's still my dad."

"Luke's been more of a father to you than Jack ever will be." Holly seemed to instantly realize she had said the wrong thing.

Lizzy's eyes narrowed as they shifted to Stone and there was something cold in them, an iciness that he found disconcerting. "Is that why you're so goddamned eager to kill him?" she demanded. "Looking to get him the fuck out of the way so you can bang his wife and play daddy to his daughter?"

"Lizzy!" Holly said sharply, horrified by her daughter's ugly words.

Stone held up his hand. "It's not about that and you know it," he said firmly. "It's about keeping you safe, nothing more, and if I have to kill your father to do that, then I will." He paused for a single heartbeat. "And I think it's going to come to that."

"What if I asked you not to? What if I asked you to let him live?"

Stone looked her dead in the eye, feeling deep affection for the young woman sitting in front of him but also the cold determination to do what needed to be done. "I'm not going to make you a promise that I might very well have to break."

TWENTY-THREE

BEFORE LIZZY COULD SAY anything more, Stone heard Rocky, his horse, snorting fiercely in his corral out back. It was possible the Appaloosa stallion was just warning off a coyote skirting along the wood line but Stone seriously doubted it. The horse was so accustomed to the coyotes and coy-wolves that roamed the property that he almost never bothered to make noise about them.

Stone said, "They're coming."

Holly's face blanched. "Are you sure?"

Outside, the stallion snorted again, and Stone nodded. "That's what Rocky is trying to tell us."

As if to confirm the point, Max's head suddenly came up and a low growl rumbled in the Shottie's throat as if to say, *We've got visitors, and they're not here to give me belly rubs or biscuits.*

Stone felt the surge of pre-combat adrenaline and welcomed it. The waiting was over. The time for action had arrived. Soon, people would be dead. Stone silently renewed his vow that the people he cared about would not be numbered among the corpses that were about to get stacked.

"Stick to the plan," he said. "Both of you go downstairs and get behind the bar. The guns are all laid out on top for you. The stairs are the only way into the basement. You see anybody but me coming down those stairs, light 'em up, and don't let off the trigger until they're good and dead." It was the same way he had survived an assault when murderous survivalists attacked his house two years ago. The bar was nestled in an alcove of the basement, surrounded by concrete walls on three sides, with the stone-faced bar providing protection on the fourth side and a direct view of the stairway. It was the best defensive position in the house.

"Where are you going to be?" Lizzy asked. She looked scared and brave at the same time. If she was still angry with him, it didn't show. Maybe the reality of the situation was setting in, making her realize that lethal force was the only option that would permanently neutralize the threat to their lives.

"Outside," Stone replied. "Making sure these bastards never get in."

"Couldn't you just stay inside, call for help, and wait for the cavalry to arrive?" Holly suggested.

"This will be over long before anybody could get here."

Holly looked grim. Not panicked, just burdened with the weight of the situation. This wasn't her first rodeo. She knew what was coming and what it would take to stay alive. She knew what Stone was going to do and she knew what she might have to do. She had killed before and would do so again without hesitation if that's what it came down to. With Lizzy's life on the line, she could explode into mama-bear rage-mode like flicking a switch.

Stone knew if the enemy outside got past him and penetrated the house, Holly would kill them all or die trying. Jack Dawson would discover that his ex-wife was no longer the meek and mild waitress he'd met in Vegas all those years ago.

As she and Lizzy walked past him toward the basement stairs, Holly placed her hand on his chest and said, "You do whatever it takes out there, but make sure you come back to us."

"Trust me," Stone said. "I'm coming back. They're not."

He gave her what was supposed to be a reassuring smile and then slipped out the door into the shadows of the dawn, armed with his weapons of choice. Holly watched him go and whispered, "I do trust you, Luke. More than you'll ever know."

———

Outside, Stone immediately switched to hunter mode, the warrior within him fully awakening. He was driven to defend his home—and the people within it—by going on the offense. He was in no mood to wait for the fight to come to him. Instead, he would take the fight to them and kick their teeth down their throats courtesy of some high-velocity lead and steel. The Stealth Hunter Performance .44 Magnum was secured in a chest rig specifically designed for large-frame revolvers.

No way in heaven or hell was he letting Holly or Lizzy die this morning. Sometimes he felt conflicted when he reverted to his old ways and switched back to killing mode, but today was not one of those days. Today, the preacher took a backseat to the warrior. Fury burned in his heart for the ones who would dare to raise a hand against an innocent mother and child, a fury that left no room for doubt, guilt, or shame.

Maybe when this was over, those emotions would surface and he would face God in prayer to ask for forgiveness, but he seriously doubted it.

Stone ghosted through the early dawn mist that shrouded the acreage on which his house was built. He didn't know how many people Dawson had mustered up for the assault, nor their precise locations, but there was no way they were better than him at moving silently through the woods.

As he reached the cover of the scotch pines and white birch saplings to the south of his house, his plan was simple: hunt them down and take them out one by one. The suppressed HK416 carbine slung across his back or the Benchmade Bedlam 860 knife clipped inside his pocket would ensure all the killing was done quietly.

He swept along the southwest perimeter of his property. His footsteps were stealthy, nearly silent, his stalking skills finely honed back in his warrior days by an instructor with Apache blood in his veins. He had crept up behind more sentries and slit their throats than he cared to count.

Yeah, there was plenty of blood on his hands and there was about to be plenty more. He had no doubt the only thing that would stop Dawson was a bullet and he would be happy to provide it.

He tried to keep his mind focused on the task at hand and not think about what would happen to Holly and Lizzy if he failed. Somehow, he didn't think Jack 'Lucky Draw' Dawson was the forgiving sort. Hell, not even prison chains had been able to stop the man from seeking his vengeance. Stone had no doubt that Holly would be killed, her death as slow and torturous as Dawson could make it. As for Lizzy... well, judging by what her father had tried to do to her once, her fate might very well be worse than death.

Not gonna happen, Stone thought. *Not on my watch.*

He moved in for the first kill.

TWENTY-FOUR

UTTERLY SILENT, Stone followed the twisting maze of game trails that zig-zagged through the thick brush, skirting rocks and stepping over rotting logs as he searched for a target. It took him less than five minutes to locate the first gunman.

The man never heard him coming. Dressed in blue jeans and a camouflage jacket, he had his back to Stone's approach, a shotgun clenched in his hands as he peered through the thorny bramble toward the house.

Not sure how much Dawson is paying you, Stone thought. *But I hope it was worth your life.*

Stone's muscles tensed, ready to launch into violent action. He drew his knife and opened it slowly to avoid any *snick!* noise as the blade locked. Then he lunged forward, left hand snaking around to cover the man's mouth and prevent any outcry while the right hand drove the knife into the side of the gunman's neck. He slashed forward, the razored edge cutting through the carotid and releasing a jet of hot blood. The shotgun fell to the ground, loosed from spasming fingers, and it was all over in about ten seconds.

Once the dead man stopped thrashing, Stone cleaned the blade on the guy's jacket, painting a messy red stripe on the camo-patterned fabric. A slight breeze rustled the underbrush and made the branches rattle together like dry bones. Tendrils of mist snaked through the thicket like the tentacles of some Lovecraftian monster.

To the east, the first rays of the sun clawed their way over the crest of the mountains. The moon still prowled the sky like a ghostly afterimage, conceding its place to the dawn but not quite ready to disappear. It was a time when darkness and light coexisted.

Stone felt right at home.

He moved through the saplings again, seeking another target.

It didn't take him long to find one. The guy was crouched beside a large boulder, holding a bolt-action deer rifle. He was facing the house, paying no attention to what was going on behind him, leaving his six vulnerable.

Stone intended to make him pay for that tactical error.

He edged closer and reached for his knife again.

Bullets ripped through the saplings near his head.

Stone flinched, dropped low, and moved sideways as shredded bits of birch wood peppered his face. He forced his muscles to remain fluid and not tense up as another salvo sliced past him, kicking up divots of dirt and moss just past his position. He cursed himself for being so focused on his initial target that he had missed the gunner on his flank.

Maybe he was getting rusty. The old Stone would never have made that mistake.

"I've got you now!" a voice whooped. "Get ready to dance with the devil, preacher!"

Remaining belly-down in the dirt and moving cautiously, Stone managed to get the HK416 off his back and into his hands. Staying as flat as possible, he rolled away from the incoming fire. When he came to a stop, he saw his original intended target looking around, unsure of what had just happened, a puzzled look on his face.

Stone erased the puzzled look with a triple-burst of 5.56mm slugs. Kicked off his feet by the impact, the instantly dead guy hit the ground with the back of his skull blown open.

He could hear the other gunman, the ambusher, barging through the brush like an enraged water buffalo. Branches cracked and snapped to announce his progress and his footsteps sounded like they were being made by an elephant. As if wanting to make sure Stone knew his exact position, the man yelled, "I'm coming for your Bible-thumping ass, you son of a bitch!"

Stone didn't wait for him to show up. Just fired at the noise, heard the *thud-thud-thud* impacts of hard bullets hitting soft flesh, followed by hurting grunts. Then a loud crash as the man went down.

"Aw…fuck me." The exclamation was full of pain, realization, and the regret of stupidity. A dying man realizing that mob money didn't spend in hell.

Stone found the guy lying on his back, blinking up at the lightening sky. He was a large man with a substantial beer belly but it wasn't beer oozing out of the bullet holes in his lower abdomen. His trembling hands clutched at the wounds as if he could stop the leaking. "Oh, god...fuck me," he moaned again.

Stone ended his suffering with a single kill-shot right between the eyes. That was about all the mercy he could muster up for a man who had tried to snuff him out. "Yeah," he rasped. "Fuck you."

Stone felt the preacher side of him tear loose from its moorings and drift away until it was nothing but a speck in his psychological makeup. It would come back when all this was over, but right now, the warrior was in control, relentless and violent, with no time for the meeker aspects of the faith. With lives on the line, he had no time for turning the other cheek or showing compassion to those who would do him harm.

There was a time for everything under the sun, the scriptures claimed. That meant there was a time to kill.

And that time was right fucking now.

———

Stone had no way of knowing how many men Dawson had rustled up to attack the house. He took out two more—another slashed throat and one knifed between the ribs and into the heart—but if there were fifty guys, he was barely making a dent in the numbers. But he seriously doubted an escaped prisoner on the run, even one with Dawson's means and connections, could come up with a sizable army on such short notice. More likely, he was using the men who had facilitated his breakout along with some local talent he had recruited to his cause, probably by promising them money he never intended to pay.

Stone had homefield advantage. He knew every nook and cranny of his thirty-acre property as well as a sizable portion of the state land that butted up against it. But what he did not know was exactly how Dawson would organize his attack. If the mob boss didn't care about taking Holly or Lizzy alive, he could just march his men up to the house and blaze away with all the guns at his disposal, hoping anyone inside would be killed by the firestorm. But if he wanted his ex-wife and daughter still breathing, he would have to go in after them or force them to come out, which would change his approach.

Stone circled to the western side of his property, skirting through the thick, mature pines behind the corral. He spotted a skittish scarecrow of a man leaning against a tree with a .357 Magnum in his hand. There were rust patches all over the revolver's finish. It looked like the gun had last been oiled when Nixon was president.

Stone didn't bother bloodying his blade or wasting a bullet. He just snuck up behind the oblivious man, grabbed his head in both hands, and gave a sharp twist that broke the neck with the crackle-crunch of a snapped twig. When Stone let go of the dead body, it crumpled to the ground like a puppet with its strings cut.

Stone moved to the edge of the woods, which were still deep in shadow, the rising sun not yet having penetrated the darkness beneath the tightly knit boughs of the pines. But the field behind his house and the lawn on either side *were* illuminated by the first light of dawn and allowed him to see something that chilled his blood.

Three groups of armed men converged on the house in a coordinated, triple-pronged strike.

TWENTY-FIVE

DESPITE THE IMMINENT danger to Holly and Lizzy, Stone knew he couldn't just charge hellbent-for-leather out into the open and start cranking off rounds like an '80s action hero in some B-grade movie. With that many guns arrayed against him, he would be cut down in moments. He needed to be decisive, not reckless.

Moving as fast as he could while still remaining silent, he circled back through the woods. He wanted to see the front of the house and figure out what, if anything, was happening there. He had a hard time believing that Dawson's forces were only sweeping in from three sides. Not having anyone posted out front would be a tactical mistake. Dawson might be a rotten son of a bitch, but he wasn't stupid.

Stone reached a pile of dirt and stone tucked into the woods just off the southeast corner of his front lawn. As he crawled toward the top, doing his best to keep the Smith & Wesson revolver strapped to his chest from scraping against the loose earth, he heard someone bellowing.

"HOLLY!"

Stone didn't recognize the voice but was willing to bet dimes to dollars that it was Jack Dawson. He reached the crest of the dirt mound and carefully peered over, raising his head just enough to get a sightline.

"Holly! I know you're in there!"

Stone recognized Dawson from the pictures he had seen. The most wanted man in America right now was standing in his driveway, braced by three black-clad men sporting SCAR assault rifles.

"Holly! That *is* what you're calling yourself now, right?" Even from one hundred meters away, Stone heard Dawson chuckle, or at least imagined he did. "Stupid name for a stupid bitch."

The only sound from inside the house was a warning bark from Max. Stone had no idea what the Shottie would do if they breached the house. He'd been rescued from an illicit dogfighting ring, but he wasn't trained as an attack dog. Still, the thought of Max's powerful jaws wrapped around Dawson's throat or chomping on his testicles brought a grim smile to Stone's lips.

The assault team on the south side was now pressed up against the house, directly beneath the living room window. On the opposite side, Stone assumed the team would be stacked up by the bathroom window, the only access point along the northern wall. The team at the back would have multiple breach points to choose from: patio doors, bedroom window, or the other living room window.

Stone rested the HK416 on top of the dirt pile and got Dawson in his sights. At this range, with this rifle, he could send a bullet screaming through the mobster's head with both his eyes closed.

He inhaled, long and deep, slowing down his breathing, getting ready to take the shot.

His finger tightened on the trigger, pressing carefully, taking up the slack.

Just one squeeze and Jack Dawson would be on his way to hell.

From the back of the house came the sound of breaking glass, followed by a terrified scream from Lizzy.

The assault team was breaching.

Son of a bitch!

Dawson lunged for the front door, making his play.

Stone pulled the trigger…

…just as one of Dawson's henchmen stepped in the way.

The bullet drilled into the gunner's left cheekbone and blew out the opposite side in a bloody explosion. He went down as if all his bones had suddenly dissolved. But he had done his job and shielded his boss. Before Stone could get his gunsights back on the primary target, Dawson made it into the house, along with his two remaining bodyguards.

Shit!

The two-man assault team on the same side as Stone heard the suppressed shot—a suppressor made a gun quieter, not silent—and looked around wildly, desperate to pinpoint his location. They died not knowing where their death had come from as Stone charged over the top of the hill with the HK rifle blasting away on full-auto, burning through half a magazine. The bullets chopped them apart, tearing ragged chunks of flesh from their bodies as they shuddered through spastic death dances.

Another gunman rounded the southwest corner of the house. Stone triggered a three-round burst that caught him in the neck and nearly shredded his head right off his shoulders.

Stone wasted no time thinking about the dead. They had come here to kill him and gotten killed instead. End of story.

He sprinted across the lawn toward the front door of his house. Two more men came around the northeast corner of the garage with pistols in their hands.

Stone nailed the first one with a double-tap to the chest that cored open his heart and lungs. But the second guy managed to pop off a pair of rounds, one of which creased Stone's left thigh. The pain made him stumble and drop to one knee, skidding across the grass. He threw himself on his right side in a full-fledged slide and triggered a rising burst that caught the target low in the guts before spreading up across his chest and face. The hammering impacts drove the gunner backward but he somehow stayed on his feet until the final bullet blew off the top of his skull.

As far as Stone knew, there was only one gunman left outside. He quickly climbed to his feet and circled around the garage to the back of the house, limping slightly from his leg wound. He spotted a man wearing a ragged hunting camo and a black beanie bolting for the woods like the hounds of hell were snarling at his heels. He had a rifle but it was slung across his back.

Stone started to raise the HK416 but lowered it a moment later. Clearly the man was one of the locals Dawson had recruited, not a professional soldier. If he'd had a change of heart and wanted out of the fight, Stone was content to let him go. He had bigger fish to fry right now.

He quickly checked his leg. The bullet had torn through the fabric of his pants and burned a shallow groove through the meat, but nothing serious. The very definition of a flesh wound. It stung like hell but he had dealt with far worse during his warrior days. This pain was minimal, easily compartmentalized.

The physical pain, that is. The mental anguish of knowing there were three killers inside his house hunting people he cared about wasn't so easy to shrug off.

———

Holly heard the clomping thud of footsteps in the house above them. For a moment, she dared to hope it was Stone returning to tell her that it was all over, that they were safe now, but then she heard a voice from her past, the voice of her own personal nightmare.

"Find them," Jack Dawson said. "They're in here somewhere. But I want them alive. If you kill them, I'll kill you. We clear on that?"

Holly heard a pair of faint, muffled affirmations.

Great, he's only got two guys with him.

Holly wondered how many men Stone had killed outside. She had no doubt there were men out there dead or dying by his hand. The man she was beginning to open up her heart to was capable of ruthless, implacable violence when the situation called for it. She also wondered if Stone was aware that Dawson and his henchmen had made it inside the house. If he knew, he would be coming with all the fury of the four horsemen of the apocalypse. If he didn't know, then they would have to fend for themselves.

Lizzy sat tucked in the corner behind the bar, arms wrapped around Max's big, scarred head. She looked worried and it pained Holly that her daughter had been through so much at such a young age. The hit put out on them by the survivalist group, the death of her friend at the hands of murderous drug dealers, her abduction and near-murder by those same drug dealers...it was all a damned heavy cross for a teenager to bear.

"We're going to be okay, honey," Holly assured her, keeping her voice low so it wouldn't carry upstairs to the intruders and give away their position. "Just stay down."

"Is Luke coming back to help us?"

"If he can, he will." Holly had absolute, unwavering faith in Stone. "But until he does, we're on our own."

"I feel trapped." Lizzy sounded breathless, on the verge of hyperventilation. "I want to get out of this house."

"Making a run for it now would be suicide," said Holly.

The footsteps on the floor above them sounded like thunder as the three men stomped around, looking for them. Holly could hear doors being kicked open, glass breaking, wood splintering. They were not being gentle in their search and she knew that roughness would be transferred to them if the bastards got their hands on them.

Max growled, a low rumble in his throat, followed by a half-snarl, half-bark. Lizzy quickly cupped a hand over his muzzle to shush him but it was too late. The dog gave her an apologetic look that seemed to say, *Sorry, couldn't help myself.*

"The bitches are downstairs," Holly heard Dawson say.

"Mom!" Lizzy sounded panicked. "We have to get out of here!"

"Holly!" Dawson called out. "Don't make me send my men down there after you or it won't end well."

"Yeah, for your men. We've got guns and a dog. You send your assholes down here, they won't be coming back up unless it's in body bags."

"Guess you found some spunk while I was in prison. Good for you. You always were a mousy little thing. Now come upstairs so we can talk things out."

"I've got nothing to say to you."

"Give yourself up and I'll let Lizzy live. Make me drag you out of the basement and I'll put a bullet in her temple."

"She's your daughter, for god's sake!"

"And you took her away from me. I never got the chance to know her, so now I don't have any emotional attachment to her. If I need to blow her brains out to teach you a lesson, then blow her brains out is exactly what I'll do. You hear me, you backstabbing bitch?"

Holly hesitated, heart hammering, thoughts racing. Different scenarios and outcomes pinballed through her mind. Maybe she should just give in to his demands, go upstairs, and pray to God that he kept his word about not killing Lizzy. He was evil, sure, but would he really murder his own daughter?

But then she remembered Jack had tried to *rape* his own daughter when she was only five years old. He was a sick, twisted bastard who would not hesitate to gun Lizzy down if it helped him get what he wanted.

To hell with him. She and Lizzy were making their stand right here.

"Yeah, I hear you," she replied. "And here's my answer—you want us, come and get us, you goddamned son of a bitch!"

"Have it your way." Dawson snarled his reply. "Just remember, I'm holding all the cards right now and your luck is about to run out. Think your boyfriend is coming to save you? He's about to find out that I've got an ace up my sleeve."

An ace? What the hell is he talking about?

The question was answered a moment later when she heard the *whump-whump-whump* sound of rotors chopping through the air as a helicopter approached the house.

"Oh, god, no..." she whispered.

And then a pair of grenades came bouncing down the stairs.

TWENTY-SIX

THE BELL 505 Jet Ranger X helicopter came swooping in from the north like a metallic bird of prey, landing struts skimming the tops of the trees, rotor wash sending dead leaves and pine needles gusting away in every direction. It banked to the right of Stone's position and he saw the figure strapped into some kind of safety harness, dangling partially out of the cabin space behind the passenger seat with a rifle in their hand.

Stone knew instantly what came next. He started running toward the woods as fast as he could, the fresh dose of adrenaline acting like a numbing agent to his leg wound. No limp, just a burst of maximum speed as he launched himself into an all-out sprint for cover.

Divots of dirt erupted behind him as the airborne gunner cut loose with a sustained tracking shot that narrowly missed. Stone felt the debris pepper his heels and it propelled him forward even faster. He made it ears, and then looked at Stone as if to say, *Sorry for sleeping on the job, man, but whatever that shit was really messed me up for a minute.*

It was a crisp November afternoon, rounding the corner toward evening, the sun settling low in the sky, golden rays streaming through the branches of the coniferous trees that lined the trail. Scores of chickadees flitted around as if to keep them company.

Lizzy had called and asked him to hike with her, which he knew was code for her wanting to talk about something. He suspected he already knew but waited patiently for her to bring up whatever was on her mind.

When she did, it was with a teenager's direct bluntness. "You killed my dad."

Stone had known it was coming, but it didn't make the words any easier to hear. "How's that make you feel?" he asked.

Lizzy shrugged. "I don't blame you. You did what you had to do."

"But?"

Another shrug. "But it still feels kind of weird to be friends with the guy who gunned down my father."

"Completely understandable," Stone said. "But I didn't have a choice. He had a gun to your head. There was no way in hell I was going to let him hurt you."

"Right," she agreed. "*He* would have killed me. *You* did whatever it took to keep me safe." She paused, hesitating, and then with a slight tremble in her voice, added, "I guess that makes you more of a father to me than he was."

Stone felt something in his heart react warmly to

her words, a loosening of the cold bonds that he some-times used to keep his emotions trapped so that he couldn't get hurt again. Shackles that would condemn him to a life of forever being alone if he didn't learn how to shake them off.

"I care about you more than you know," he said. "Whatever you need me for, I'll be there."

Lizzy kicked at a rock while Max splashed through a puddle of brackish water, her eyes downcast. "And what if I need a dad?" she asked quietly.

"Do you remember how many times you've told me that I'm *not* your dad?" Stone smiled to take any edge off the words.

"I know, I know." Lizzy looked up and smiled back at him. "What can I say? I'm a teenage girl. We're complicated creatures who change our minds a lot."

Stone turned his head away from her, gazing out across the bog as the shadows darkened the water, not wanting her to see the glistening in his eyes. Not because of what she had said or what she was asking, but because it reminded him of his daughter and everything he had lost.

When he looked back at her, she was still smiling at him. She linked her arm through his with the comfort of familiarity, leaned her head against his shoulder, and said, "Thanks for saving my ass the other day. You're starting to make it a habit." She gave his arm a squeeze. "I know you're not my dad, but I love you anyway."

"I love you, too, Liz."

Her smile widened. "Now you just need to find the guts to say that to my mom."

Stone grinned and shook his head. "One step at a time, kiddo."

———

After dropping Lizzy off at home, Stone headed to the Jack Lumber Bar & Grill. It was Friday night and the place was hopping. The crowd consisted of mostly locals but there were a few unfamiliar faces sprinkled in, probably out-of-town hunters visiting the mountainous region in the hopes of bagging a big whitetail buck. Despite the murders and violence of the past week, it looked like the town was bound and determined to get back to normal. The rock 'n' roll blared, the booze flowed, and everybody seemed to be having a good time.

He looked around but didn't see Holly, but no surprise there, as fashionably late was pretty much her default setting. By now he expected it and accepted it as one of her quirks. He made his way to the bar, nodded at Grizzle who was far too busy to engage in chit-chat, and ordered his usual Jack and Coke, lots of ice, easy on the Jack. He sipped it while making small talk with the handful of people who took the time to approach him, but for the most part, everyone left him alone.

When Holly arrived, she ordered a glass of white wine and they managed to find an empty booth in the back corner, bathed in the colorful neon glow of the nearby jukebox as it cranked out '80s hair metal hits.

"How'd your walk-and-talk with Lizzy go?" she asked as soon as they sat down.

"That really what you want to talk about?"

She blushed ever so slightly and traced a finger along the rim of her wineglass. "Maybe we should just forget about what happened that night." She sighed and smiled at him. "I acted like a brazen hussy and you turned me down."

"Trust me, it was hard."

Holly smirked. "Oh, it was hard, all right."

It had been a long time since Stone had blushed but he felt warmth spread across his cheeks. He shook his head and grinned. "You're incorrigible."

Holly reached a hand across the table and touched his forearm. "Let's just forget it happened—or rather, *almost* happened—and move on. Like you said that night, I was scared and looking for comfort. It was the wrong time and I'm sorry I let it happen."

Stone put his hand on top of hers, looked deep into her eyes, and quietly asked, "Think there'll ever be a right time?"

She didn't say anything for several long heartbeats, seemingly content to sit there with his hand on hers and their gazes locked together. Finally, she said, "I guess only God knows, but I hope so."

A drunken dancer ricocheted off her partner and banged into the table, causing their drinks to slosh over the sides of their glasses. She immediately giggled, fired off a quick "Sorry!" and gyrated back into the fray before the song ended.

Stone and Holly, the serious mood broken, laughed and went back to their drinks. As they talked about topics that didn't force them to tap-dance around emotional landmines, Stone found a solemn corner of his mind mulling over all that had happened since he drove his Blazer into this small mountain town. He had come here with more than his fair share of scars, both from his warrior days and the unexpected death of his daughter, but Holly and Lizzy's presence in his life had gone a long way toward healing those wounds.

Maybe someday they would heal completely, and he would truly be happy again. Maybe someday, two cautious, guarded hearts would be able to lower their defenses all the way and mend each other for good. Maybe someday they wouldn't talk about waiting for the right time, because maybe someday it would actually *be* the right time.

So many maybes.

But the maybes were worth waiting for, and Stone knew better than most how to be patient and let things unfold in God's own timing. Until then, he would continue to use both the Bible and gun to keep the peace in Whisper Falls, and he would never stop raining fury down on anyone who came to this town with evil intentions.

Because matters of the heart could wait.

Justice could not.

A LOOK AT: THE ASSASSIN'S PRAYER

THE ASSASSINS BOOK ONE

HARD-HITTING ACTION WITH A WHOLE LOT OF HEART.

Burned by the betrayal of his best friend and embittered by the tragic death of his wife, former government assassin Gabriel Asher becomes a freelance gun-for-hire, trying hard to bury the past beneath a violent sea of bullets, blood, and booze.

But some sins refuse to stay buried…

Asher soon finds himself targeted by Black Talon, a brutal kill-team from his past led by the ruthless and legendary Colonel Macklin. Asher just wants to be left alone but when fate thrusts an ex-lover back into his life and she is caught up in the crossfire, Asher unleashes a take-no-prisoners war against his enemies. As the guns thunder and the bodies bite the dust, he finds the scars on his soul being ripped wide open.

With its full-throttle pace, hard-hitting action, and heart-wrenching emotion, The Assassin's Prayer is a relentless tale of redemption for those who know that sometimes bullets speak louder than words.

Publisher's Note: The Assassin's Prayer has been updated with new characters, major revisions, and an exhilarating new ending in this brand-new edition.

AVAILABLE NOW

ABOUT THE AUTHOR

Mark Allen was raised by an ancient clan of ruthless ninjas and now that he has revealed this dark secret, he will most likely be dead by tomorrow for breaking the sacred oath of silence. The ninjas take this stuff very seriously.

When not practicing his shuriken-throwing techniques or browsing flea markets for a new katana, Mark writes action fiction. He prefers his pose to pack a punch, likes his heroes to sport twin Micro-Uzis a la Chuck Norris in Invasion USA, and firmly believes there is no such thing as too many headshots in a novel.

He started writing "guns 'n' guts" (his term for the action genre) at the not-so-tender age of 16 and soon won his first regional short story contest. His debut action novel, The Assassin's Prayer, was optioned by Showtime for a direct-to-cable movie. When that didn't pan out, he published the book on Amazon to great success, moving over 10,000 copies in its first year, thanks to its visceral combination of raw, redemptive drama mixed with unflinching violence.

Now, as part of the Wolfpack team, Mark Allen looks forward to bringing his bloody brand of gun-slinging, bullet-blasting mayhem to the action-reading masses.

Mark currently resides in the Adirondack Mountains of upstate New York with a wife who doubts his ninja skills because he's always slicing his fingers while chopping veggies, two daughters who refuse to take tae kwon do, let alone ninjitsu, and enough firepower to ensure that he is never bothered by door-to-door salesmen.

9 781639 775248